The
Paths
We Walk

a novel
by
Mary Arnold

ISBN: 9798443246161

Cover by Rossano Designs

For Nate, Emma, Jacob, and Claire
With all my love

Psalm 127: 1 a
Unless the LORD builds the house,
those who build it labor in vain.

Prologue

August 1951

The warm, Texas sun had already heated the breezeless August afternoon air into a crackling inferno. Heat waves shimmered just above the sidewalk pavement warning pedestrians to hurry to their destinations.

Christine Hinkle entered Frank's Diner, a local hang-out favored by even the hippest kids from both of the nearby high schools. From the lunch counter, Ms. Shirley, the co-owner, greeted her with a friendly wave and a "Howdy, girl." Christine smiled and returned the wave, then headed to her friends' favorite booth in the back corner. It was the perfect location to see everyone who entered the diner while guarding their secrets from others' ears.

Christine sank down into the familiar, leather cushions knowing that she and her friends were on the cusp of new beginnings and wanting to have just a few moments longer of the way things had always been.

The bell on the door jingled, announcing the entrance of Patty—Patricia, as she wanted to go by now, at least when she was at work. She claimed it was more mature, a name fit for a young woman in business school. Patty glided toward the table. Christine could tell she was trying to perfect her Doris Day walk again. She rolled her eyes then giggled. The other day they had been over at Patty's house, practicing how to act sophisticated, in case they met an extremely urbane man or a motion picture recruiter. One never knew when such skills might be needed, after all. They had ended up with a mess of dresses to clean off the floor and the urge to go shopping for clothing more refined and appropriate for their new status as career women. Well, almost career women. Once they completed their two year business training courses, they would be independent, educated women with successful jobs.

"Whew, this heat," Patty said, wiping her sweat-moistened forehead. "I keep telling Daddy he needs to invest in an in-ground swimming pool for the backyard. You know him: 'If it's on your dime, kid, sure, because it won't be on mine,'" Patty mimicked her father's teasing, stern tone and added a dramatic wink as Mr. Meyer was known to do.

A soft giggle sounded from behind as Megan Freemont, Meg to her friends, slid into the booth beside Christine. Meg rounded out today's trio.

"Hi, girls." Meg's soothing southern drawl twanged. "Are ya'll feeling excited but sad at the same time? Maybe it's just me. Seems like it was just days ago that we were barely surviving Biology class and having Sheila tutor us through Algebra and Chemistry. Now, here we are saying our first real goodbye. I feel like it's the end of an era. At least you two are sticking close together. With ya'll having known one another since infancy, I can imagine it would be so much harder to even think about moving away." Meg looked tearful.

Ms. Shirley walked over then, interrupting the gloom that had begun to settle over the girls. "Milk shakes for everyone, it is?" Ms. Shirley questioned good naturedly. The young women nodded in agreement.

"Sure is different seeing you three without Sheila. I bet she's giving them Yankees a big taste of Southern spunk about now." Ms. Shirley gave them a wide grin at the thought.

The girls laughed. Christine imagined that Ms. Shirley was quite right about their friend. She pictured Sheila. Since childhood, their brilliant and brassy friend had led their little group. Whatever came their way, Sheila was at the forefront. It was hard to imagine the next four years without Sheila getting them into scrapes or signing them up for some volunteer project. After Sheila's valedictorian speech at graduation, it had struck Christine that her friend would accomplish big goals. Sheila was a rising star if there ever was one. Like Ms. Shirley, Christine would bet on Sheila's ability to turn the whole Northwestern University science department on their heads.

As they sipped their cool, creamy drinks, the girls reminisced about their years at their recent alma mater, Arlington Heights High School. They retold their favorite stories and shared what they knew about their classmates, some like Sheila and Meg, who were off to university and others who were getting married or entering the workforce.

"Gee, it's Antsville in here. You'd think the whole town has nothing better to do than to stop by for a fountain drink." Meg's cousin, Nelson Richards, joined them squeezing into the booth next to Patty, which was not an easy feat for his six foot two lanky frame. "Y'all hear that Andrew Bates joined up? He had deferment served up to him on a silver platter, and he's off to Korea instead," Nelson said.

Christine glanced at Patty as Nelson droned on about the conflict in Korea and politics. Patty's cheerful grin had been replaced with a firm line. She knew firsthand how young men went exuberantly off to war, claiming they would whip the enemy in no time, only to come home broken in body and spirit. Six years later, her brother, Scott, was still waging war in his mind over what he had done in the South Pacific. Patty did not like to talk about Scott's struggles or war, but Christine knew both subjects weighed heavily on her heart and mind.

Had Sheila been there, she would have grabbed Nelson by the hand and taken him for a turn to whatever song was being played on the jukebox in the corner. Within minutes, they would be laughing or focused on some crusade to save or enliven the citizens of Fort Worth.

Christine chided herself to break through Nelson's discouraging monologue. This was supposed to be a celebration of their new chapter in life, not a time to get mired in things they could not change today. She wanted to redeem their last moments together because some feeling told her that things would never be quite the same again.

In fact, tomorrow morning, Meg and Nelson would drive to Ole' Miss to begin their college studies. Patty had already begun a typist job at her uncle's law practice and would start business school classes with Christine in a few days. Things were definitely changing, which both thrilled and terrified Christine. She embraced change in most areas of her life, but this divergence of their paths was a little unsettling, to be honest.

"Jimmy Stewart is by far the best actor. Don't you agree, Christine?" Patty argued playfully with Meg. Their banter broke Christine from her reverie.

"Of course, although you know I would gladly listen to Cary Grant sweet talk me any day," Meg replied. Their group couldn't get enough of Stewart's and Grant's films and were enamored with the suave actors.

"As much as I love Jimmy Stewart and Cary Grant, ladies, let us not forget to mention gorgeous Gregory Peck, handsome Henry Fonda, and beautiful Bing Crosby. We love them too after all." Christine joined along in their fun, a tiny spiteful part of her happy to see Nelson squirm a bit. That is what he got for being a storm cloud on their sunny fun afternoon together.

Nelson rolled his eyes at their girlish chatter and headed to the lunch counter with an "I'll see you gals." Patty and Christine waved half-heartedly when Nelson turned back to look at them once more before taking a seat at one of the counter's high stools.

A half hour later, Patty linked arms with Christine as they walked to the block where they had grown up just three houses apart. Patty hesitated before saying, "It was a good afternoon. Though, when Nelson began talking about Korea and Andrew joining up, I near fainted, and not from the heat, mind you. Andrew has always been so thoughtful and kind, especially considering he comes from one of Fort Worth's most moneyed families. I would hate to see him get hurt or worse."

It was the closest Patty had ever come to admitting her crush on Andrew Bates. Sure, she had liked different boys in their class throughout the years, but Andrew seemed to be in a category of his own. Christine had known Patty's crush since Eighth Grade, but Patty kept this secret close, even from her best friend since their church nursery days.

She had wondered about Patty's infatuation throughout the years. Andrew and Patty were quite opposite in many ways. Yet, she has resolved to be patient. Knowing her friend as well as she did, Christine knew Patty would share her heart on the matter when she wanted to. And she would be ready for all the juicy details if that time ever came.

The last few bungalows stood before them sooner than wished. An unnamed feeling swelled through Christine. She wondered if Patty felt it too. Though Christine and Patty walked back to the same houses they left mere hours earlier, it was as if they had crossed over the threshold between the days of childhood and those of an adult. Gone were the days of cutting out paper dolls and braiding hair, as were those of being paper shakers at school pep rallies or Friday night dances waiting on the wall together for one of the boys to wipe off his sweat slick hands and get the nerve to ask for a dance. They had passed English Literature with honors and Chemistry, remarkably, without blowing up the science lab. Even their high school graduation was three months past. Now, they would be walking the halls of higher education and joining the working crowd.

Christine and Patty said their goodbyes with an "I'll see you Sunday," and a wave. Christine was excited, but felt like she could cry at the same time. However, as her grandmother always said, "You can only walk forward through time. Best get to it." Christine would. She vowed to embrace her future and make it a grand one.

Not for the first time in his life, Dennis Oswald was broke. As in, he would consider himself lucky to have a quarter to his name, even though pay day was still four days away. *Broke again.* It was always empty blue jean pockets and an even emptier belly. He sighed. It would be saltine crackers and an apple for supper again tonight. Luckily, they had been on sale at the store this week, or he might have had to go without a meal or two.

Dennis dusted his hands off on his blue jeans and followed the other shift workers away from the production line where they worked at the Purina Mills factory, just east of downtown Fort Worth. He walked outside into sunlight so bright he saw black dots for a moment. Of course, the dots could be from the hunger that had clawed at his middle since his meager lunch was just as lousy as he expected dinner to be.

In the parking lot, Jerry revved the engine on his old, beat up Ford truck. It was his signal to the other linemen to jump in or be stuck walking home in the near one hundred degree heat. Dennis jogged over to hitch a ride with Jerry, Dusty, and whoever else could squeeze into the back truck bed. As Jerry's friends and roommates, Dennis and Dusty got to ride in the cab as long as they showed up in time. Jerry was not a particularly patient man, so Dennis knew to head out straight after the end of shift whistle blew.

Dennis winced just thinking back to the time Jerry made good on his threat. Last February, Dusty had started lollygagging and talking too long while clocking out a few days in a row. Though they had known one another since boyhood, Jerry left Dusty behind despite the frigid temperatures outside. It had not been a pleasant evening once Dusty got home. Dennis hated that he and Craig had to hold Dusty down so he didn't beat the snot out of Jerry. Neither man had apologized to the other but both had managed to cool down enough for the little house to regain the strained equilibrium it usually operated in. Dennis dreaded the tension that always seemed to be hanging overhead.

This afternoon, Dennis compressed his nearly six foot frame into the cab and made room for Dusty, who worked on the other side of the line from Jerry and Dennis. The August sun beat down on the metal roof, making the inside seem like they were in a blazing conflagration, instead of offering a little relief. The truck bed would have a breeze, but it also would include a bug or two in the face. Thus, Dennis took the proffered seat in the cab.

Jerry drove the way he lived his life in general: fast and hard. They bumped along and took turns and curves more rapidly than anyone should. Dennis wondered how the guys riding in the back stayed in at times. Had he not been given a spot in the cab, Dennis doubted the risk each ride presented would be worth it. A few of the guys from the back were dropped off at a corner before Jerry pulled the truck to a lurching stop in front of the small shack of a house they and their fourth roommate, Craig, shared.

Dennis sat and waited for Dusty to slide out the truck so he could exit. "You coming in?" Dusty leaned around Dennis to ask Jerry as he extricated his stocky form from the truck seat.

"Nah, I got to go see Sherry. She's mad at me for some reason or another again. Told her I would stop by, and I ain't spending my whole night at that diner," Jerry replied.

It was hard to keep up, but Dennis recalled that Sherry was Jerry's girl this month. Dusty smirked and called out a "Good luck," as he lumbered into the house. Dusty loved saying, "Sherry and Jerry" in an immature, singsong tone when Jerry was not around. He was just smart enough to know he would be pulling knuckles off his face if he teased Jerry.

Inside their sardine can of a living room, Dusty threw himself down on the musty sofa he and Craig had recovered from the side of the road one night last winter. It was a faded and lumpy, old thing in an odd shade of brown, but was arguably the highest quality piece of furniture in their entire place.

"What a day! Reynolds was on my case the whole time. There's no pleasing him. Can't see how we can go any faster," Dusty complained as he peeled off his dirty socks and tossed them at some unknown destination. Dusty reached for the box of cereal he had left on the floor after its last use and began to munch happily on the dry Sugar Crisps.

Craig trudged in just then, stinking of gasoline from his job at the filling station. "Hey, y'all. I brought the mail in," Craig said. He handed Dennis two envelopes. The giant of a man wore a dopey grin on his face most of the time, but Dennis preferred it over Jerry's womanizing leer and brash ways and Dusty's grumpy whining. Not that the other guys were all bad; Jerry had offered Dennis cheap rent in their house when he had nowhere to go last summer, and Dusty occasionally shared his canned sausages or sardines with Dennis. He cringed at the smell of them both, but he was too desperate to resist the offer when it came; plus, there was no sense in offending Dusty unnecessarily.

They were a ragtag group. Jerry and Dusty grew up together in some small town out in west Texas and had come to Fort Worth in search of work a few years earlier. Two years ago, Craig had met Jerry through his cousin, Jerry's girl of the month at the time. He moved in the week after. Craig was laid back and easy to get along with, which

9

is why he stayed, even though his cousin had been dumped in Jerry's pursuit of the perfect woman. Nine months later, Dennis was invited because Jerry wanted to minimize his rent payment.

Dennis knew he could be living in a whole lot worse of conditions. He had at times the past few years. So here he sat on the chair with the torn fabric and abnormal odor and chose to be thankful for what he had.

Not thirty minutes after he dropped them off, Jerry burst through the front door looking angrier than a rodeo bull. He smelled like one too. The reeking scent of animal feed trailed behind many of the guys long after they left the production line for the day. Dennis supposed he did not smell much better. Although he would have advised Jerry to take a shower before seeing his girl, if the guy actually cared what he thought.

"Sherry is a fool. She ignored me and kept seating everyone else. I said, 'What's the idea?' and she told me not to come see her again. Then, she got the cook out, and he was madder than all get out. Don't know what I did but she ain't worth the trouble. Won't keep me from eatin' at the diner though. I'm not going to let her tell me what to do." Jerry shoved Dusty's legs off and sat down hard on the couch. Dennis and Craig kept silent. If Pop had taught him one thing, it was that a smart man knew when to keep his peace. He had learned that one had to be smart to survive this crazy life.

Dusty made a few derogatory remarks about Sherry, cereal bits spraying out of his mouth the more worked up he got. Dennis was almost certain that Dusty had met Sherry all of one time, but that did not stop him from maligning her looks and character.

Dennis wished he would shut up. He would go into the other room but it didn't matter with the walls being so paper thin. He might as well stay where he was at and keep Dusty and Jerry from turning on him. He had learned that if a guy sat there quietly for long enough, he was less likely to be noticed and get pulled into the melee.

So Dennis sat listening to the barrage of ugly words. It took him back to memories of his childhood; a place he swore he would never purposely go. He clenched his fists. Something had to change. Working a go nowhere job, barely making enough to feed, clothe, and save a little, and listening to the same kind of ugly his father spewed was not the life Dennis envisioned or desired for himself.

For the past three years, he had spent every last penny trying to work his way through college, taking one night class at a time. As a young teen, Dennis had determined to prove his old man wrong, and had been working at it, slowly chipping away at his degree. He was a few credits short of an associates' degree; however, his money and luck had run out. Dennis had taken all of the evening courses his program offered, and he would have no money to pay for daytime classes or anything else if he quit his job in order to take the required courses.

Dennis sat in the dirty arm chair to the side of Dusty and wondered *How could a guy feel so old at twenty-one?* He was tired and worn down from too little food, too often, and from being around such ugliness one time too many.

He would not call himself an optimist by any means. He had seen too much and had lived too hard of a life in his short number of years. However, Dennis liked to think that there was more to this life for those who worked hard to get it.

Getting a second job was one solution, but Dennis knew that he could barely keep up with work and school as it was. More and more guys from the line at work were quitting and joining the fight in Korea. Dennis had no desire to fight any enemy in a foreign land. Few places these days were hiring guys with his kind of skills or level of education. He had given what he had managed to save to ensure that his sister, Janet, got out of a bad situation. She needed a place where she could live safely, until she found work somewhere far away from her abusive boyfriend, Calvin, and their equally brutal father.

When he could take no more of his roommates' antics, Dennis went to the room he shared with Craig. Earlier, he had tossed his mail on his bunk without looking at them. *Best see what they say before I misplace them.* The first was from the college reminding him to register and pay for his fall classes. He put it to the side, frustrated that he could do neither at this time. The next piece of mail read U.S. Selective Service Board in the top left corner. He stared at it, a feeling of dread welling up inside his chest. He slit the top and pulled out an official looking letter. He was being drafted into the Army. *Drafted!*

Suddenly, the small room felt like a prison cell. He had to get out of there. In less than a minute he was out of the house and onto the street walking with no destination in mind. He honestly didn't care where he went.

Dennis wandered aimlessly until the aromas from a nearby restaurant made his stomach grumble. He glanced over to see the joint's name and grimaced at the irony before him. One door over from the restaurant's entry was a U.S. military recruitment office. The one place he had hoped to avoid was right in front of him. The Army promised three meals a day and assistance with college tuition, or so said the poster outside the recruitment office. Dennis turned the bit of news around in his mind. He would have a lot of risk and hard work to get those benefits, but his options were few right now anyway. He walked back home— uncertainty gripping his thoughts.

Craig greeted him from the kitchen when he came in the front door. The smell of the grilled cheese sandwich he was frying made Dennis's mouth water, but he knew there would be nothing as grand for his supper. Dennis looked over at Jerry who was still on the couch and appeared to be in the same foul mood as when he had left. Dusty had fallen asleep in the chair clasping an empty bottle with two more lying on the floor next to him. Dennis could feel the weight of hard living beginning to drag him under. Something told him life had to better than what he was living like now. Change was the only way he would make it out from this hole. Right now, the Army was the solution that presented itself. He had to move forward before he lost the will to.

A day later, Dennis took time off work and reported to the military induction office. The lobby was chock-full of U.S. Army, Air Force, Marine Corps, and Navy posters that made everything seem like the military was the way to see the world, a grand adventure of sorts. Dennis wavered at the thought. This would be no holiday vacation—not that he had ever taken a vacation to know.

He gathered his courage, straightened his back, and marched through the office door. The induction officer sent him to be given both psychological and physical exams.

The military doctor examined him with a sharp eye. "Too skinny," he barked out.

Dennis figured as much. "What do I have to do to remedy that, sir?" he questioned humbly. *What would he do if he was unfit for service?* His future hinged on the doctor's decision. Dennis's pulse sped up as he waited for the man to answer.

"Put on about ten pounds, son," he was directed.

Ten pounds could take an eternity to gain based on his meal budget. Dennis licked his lips; trying to phrase his next question without sounding desperate. Silence hung heavily in the cramped room. Dennis rubbed the back of his neck and shuffled his feet. He could not give up easily. If he was one who gave into fear or accepted being told "no" when he'd set his mind to something, Dennis would have turned out like his pop long before now. Being like Pop was not a path Dennis wanted to take.

The doctor glanced up at him again, seeming a little pleased that Dennis had stuck around. "Look, kid, they need to fill this enlistment group soon. Draftees have to ship out to basic training camp in three weeks. If you can gain at least five pounds by then, I can clear you."

Dennis nodded. He was grateful for a chance—even if it was a long shot. "Be back in here by the twenty-first to report for camp," the doctor said as Dennis turned to walk out the door. "Son, here, get yourself a decent meal or two." The older man pushed three crisp dollar bills into Dennis's hand and opened the door for him.

Dennis spent the following two weeks eating better than he had in over a year. He was determined not to be detoured. He had set his course in motion and would see it through. He figured if he survived boot camp and the two years of compulsory service, he could use the tuition assistance or get a job that paid better; lots of places liked to hire Army veterans.

Dennis gained seven pounds in those two weeks. He found that it was not hard if a man spent all his money, minus rent, on food. It had been good to eat more than a few bites again. Dennis had even allowed himself to indulge in a slice of pie at the diner. It cost him more than he had paid for a day's worth of meals most weeks before, but the creamy treat had been worth every penny. Eating that piece of custard pie had been like heaven for a few minutes; he might even have imagined that he heard the angels plucking away on their harps.

When he was certain he could make the cut, Dennis gave his boss at Purina his notice. It was one week less than required, but that was all he had to spare. Ronald was a fair foreman and told him he hated to see him go, but understood when a man felt called to do his duty for his country. Dennis bobbled his head in agreement, all the while wishing it was noble patriotism instead of hunger and world weariness that drove him.

His last night at the house, Craig and the guys gave Dennis a send off of sorts. They were all home, which was rare, due to Jerry's dating schedule. They sat around and talked and ate fried pies Craig brought home from the filling station. It was a night of camaraderie they rarely experienced. Jerry and Dusty didn't even pick a fight with each other once the whole evening.

Dennis said his goodbyes around midnight and went to bed, though he doubted sleep would come. As he lay in bed, he hoped he was not making the biggest mistake of his life. Last week, Jerry had asked him if he wanted to find a way to get out the mandatory service. Even Dusty seemed a little hesitant at the idea of Dennis going off to war. He wished he had other options.

Early the next morning, he stuffed the remainder of his few possessions into the Army issued duffle bag and took the bus to the induction office. As he scrambled into the back of the Army truck bound for basic training camp, Dennis looked at the city he had never left but one other time in all his years. It was a sleepy little town where little excitement happened unless one went looking for it. Fort Worth was where some of his best and worst days had been lived. It was frightening if he let himself dwell on leaving the familiar to go to unknown destinations and face battle. He certainly would miss the comfort of only home he had ever known. With a shake of his head, he attempted to focus on nothing more than the road ahead of him.

Chapter 1

March 1955

"Bedford and Evans Dentistry, this is Christine. How may I help you?" Christine answered.

Bryan's commanding voice filled the line. "Christine, Mother told me to remind you that our reservation for dinner at the club are promptly at six o'clock tonight. She also wants you to wear your pastel yellow dress because she and Barbara are wearing blue and green and that will compliment their ensemble."

Christine grimaced. Pastel yellow washed out her pale complexion. Mrs. Wharton, who was quite the fashion mogul of her social set, surely would have considered that when she purchased the dress for Christine a few months before. This was a thought pattern that was best not spending too much time thinking on, or Christine would feel her normally calm personality flare to life with frustration.

Christine tried to keep the irritation from her voice; he was only the messenger after all. "Yes, Bryan. I will have to meet you at the club because we are running a little behind schedule today," she said softly, hoping to avoid his annoyance.

A long suffering sigh came across the wire. "You know I prefer to pick you up and that we ride together," he replied. "Hold on, then." Christine heard murmuring in the background, though Bryan must have covered the telephone receiver.

"That will do for today, but let's try not to make it a habit. You know it bothers mother." He stopped and added more gently, "Hold on a minute, Christine." Bryan said something to his secretary again and then finished his thought. "Charles and I are playing doubles against Brooks and his new law assistant. Should be easy enough to wipe the court with them, but now I can prolong their misery," he said in a competitive manner. "I'll meet you at the front foyer, and we will walk in together. Got to run." The line clicked off.

Christine frowned at the paperwork remaining on her desk. How long would Bryan be put out by the change in plans? Was the thought of victory on the court enough to derail his animosity toward her imagined imposition?

"Hello, dear, I am here for my eleven o'clock appointment with Dr. Bedford."

"Good morning, Mrs. Jensen." Christine greeted the elderly woman with a smile.

The afternoon hours passed quickly as one patient after another came and left. After Dr. Evans walked their last patient of the day to the door, he commented, "It's quite the downpour out there," as he came back to the reception desk. "Mr. Davis was our final appointment. Why don't we all go home before it gets too dark? I don't know that this weather is going to lighten up any time soon. Paperwork can wait until tomorrow."

Dr. Bedford joined them in the office foyer, handing out umbrellas. "I have not seen it rain like this in years," he said, staring out the window at the rain pouring off the building's awnings. "Drive safely; I will see you both in the morning." With that he dashed through the rain, his figure quickly enveloped in the fog and torrential shower.

On the drive home, Christine debated about calling Bryan to inform him that he could pick her up. With the sudden rainstorm changing his plans, who knew whether he had decided to play an indoor game at the club or go home to dress for dinner. Attempting to alter their plans at this point was most likely more hassle than it was worth. It was too bad that the sunny, spring-like morning had given way to the dark clouds and heavy downpour.

As Christine ironed the pastel yellow dress and readied herself for dinner with Bryan, his sister Barbara, and the ever-formidable Mrs. Wharton, rain continued to pelt the roof of the garage apartment she shared with Patty. She thought about the evening ahead, mentally preparing herself for what was to come. She was one of five children from a household where supper time was a loud, boisterous affair. Tonight's dinner would be quite the opposite. The country club's dining room boasted of lush carpet against dark wood, paneled walls. Elegant drapery ensconced large windows with expansive views of the golf course's oak lined fairways. Members spoke in low, hushed tones giving an air of sophistication and retreat. Even the wait staff slipped in and out like mice, as if worried that one loud movement would catch a cat's watchful eye. Christine appreciated the luxury of it all and the honor of being a guest of the esteemed Wharton family, but felt it came with a price that she was unsure she wanted to pay.

It was a little less than a year ago that Christine had first been invited to dine at the club with the Wharton family. Christine and Bryan had been seeing each other for six months by that time. The invitation from Mrs. Wharton had come through Bryan. He delivered it with a pleased look and the expectation for it to be accepted without reservation. Christine had been thrilled at it initially, until nerves began to set in. Though she had dined at the club multiple times and attended several society events with the family since that first dinner, Christine still experienced a tremor of nerves as she thought about walking through the columned entrance again. The impressive environment no longer intimidated her, but the Wharton's formal conversation was stiff; if truth be told, it was exhausting.

She checked her nylons for runs and searched for her silver barrette while continuing to contemplate her and Bryan's relationship. At times, she felt the void between their different backgrounds and personalities seemed immense. While he lived in a sprawling family home on a bluff overlooking the Trinity River, Christine came from an ordinary house nearly bursting at the seams with children while she and her siblings were in their younger years. Bryan's mother had high expectations for her children and was rarely affectionate from what Christine had witnessed. His father had passed in Bryan's adolescence but had been depicted as austere and old fashioned. Bryan was straight laced in most aspects. He was fiercely competitive and tenacious when he wanted something. These qualities served him well as he cross examined a witness in court, no doubt. She had once found the features attractive, but lately they were beginning to wear on her nerves. Her family was of modest means, and loved each other well and deeply. They saw no need or desire to pretend to be anything other than what they were. Although they may never have some of the luxurious possessions others enjoyed, her parents instilled a strong work ethic and thankfulness to the good Lord in their children, and that felt like enough at the end of the day. Being the product of two such parents, Christine strove to do her best at what she put her mind to. She enjoyed organization and details but knew that flexibility and compromise were part of a balanced life. Bryan thrived on keeping an audience captive with his natural charisma, whereas Christine was a behind the scenes person who calmly completed the tasks she needed to without fanfare. It was not that Christine did not appreciate recognition or fun; she just preferred to have them in laid back, smaller social settings.

While she donned the yellow chiffon dress and searched for her matching pumps, Christine recollected how they had met at a charity dance Meg Freemont had invited her to. Meg seemed to grin like the Cheshire Cat after she saw Christine dance with the motion picture star handsome man. Later, Meg pulled Christine behind a large, potted plant to whisper about how jealous all the other unattached females were that one of Fort Worth's most eligible bachelors crossed the crowded dance floor specifically to introduce himself to her. What Bryan had seen from across the packed room still puzzled her. She possessed a cute, round face with a perky nose that she was rather fond of, but her dress had been from Montgomery Ward, not Bloomingdales. Christine had long since accepted that all the coeds at the dance questioned, "Why her?" A year ago, she had determined to stop playing that broken record and enjoy the path she was on.

Snapping out of her musings, Christine took another critical look at the simple yet elegant chignon she had swept her brown hair into. It was not perfect, but would have to do given the time and the rain. Christine jotted a quick note to Patty asking her to take the trash to the curb when the rain stopped. Mrs. Anderson, the landlord of their tiny apartment did not like it when they missed trash day. She insisted that proper tenants must adhere to a schedule or they would be given a formal warning. The next step was a citation and review of their rental agreement. In the almost two years of renting from Mrs. Anderson, the girls had yet to earn such a demerit but the threat of one always loomed.

The dark sky continued to unleash torrents of rain down as Christine dashed to her car, dodging large puddles of water. Thankfully, she would have plenty of time to make it to Bryan's requested location.

Once on the road, Christine's windshield wipers strained against the onslaught of wind and water. Slowly, steadily, she made her way through the darkened city streets. Street lamps glowed but barely pierced the tempest. Christine gripped the steering wheel, as if she could release a little of her growing fear of the storm's potency into the soft leather. "Just a few minutes more," she chanted repeatedly, trying to rally herself. Up ahead, a bus was stopped to let off and pick up more passengers. *Poor souls.*

Chapter 2

March 1955

Dennis Oswald used to think Kay was the life of the party. She was all gold and glitz, her white teeth flashing as much as the cubic zirconium earrings she wore. Laughter and a good time were synonymous with Kay. Why, then, did she annoy him so much these days? It seemed like all she did was whine and moan or cry and yell at him. In Kay's eyes, he did not bring in enough money from his job at the bank. He was too emotionally distant or too dull when she expected life to be one constant engaging source of entertainment. He was too serious and on her case all the time because she could not live up to his "extreme" expectations—like that she save a few dollars from each paycheck or help with the laundry instead of going out all the time. Since he tried to be a docile, unassuming guy, who did his best to live at peace with everyone, all her accusations had really started to eat at him.

However, this Monday afternoon, Dennis had felt a spark of excitement when Kay called him up at work and asked him to join her at Frank's Diner for a quick supper right after work. Frank's was their place. They'd a lot of good times there. The first time Dennis had seen Kay was in the center booth of Frank's. She had been laughing. Then their eyes met across the room, and she had given him her million dollar smile. She got up from the booth, leaving the men surrounding her sitting there stunned by her abrupt departure. As Kay made her way across the short space, heads turned to take her in. The combination of her style and looks and effervescent personality was truly magnificent to behold. She approached his seat at the counter and had put her hand on Dennis's shoulder and leaned close, introducing herself. Dennis knew that every guy in the joint was jealous of him.

From then on, there had been house parties, dancing at night clubs, or one exciting outing after another. Dennis had been caught in the whirlwind of such a life. Before the Army, his life had consisted of trying to make a buck to survive. As an enlisted private in the Army whose job was to carry the wounded out of battle on liters, life had been much of the same vein: keep your head down and stay alive. Freshly discharged from the Army just two months earlier, Dennis was still adjusting to a normal life with the first decent job he had ever had. Then, here came the glamorous Kay who dazzled him with her quest to have fun and invite everyone along for the ride. Kay was a sales girl, and sometimes a model, at Montgomery Ward. She was fashionable and was well liked wherever they went.

Last year, on a whim, they had gone to the Justice of the Peace and got married. What had started out as a lark spurred on by a current of too many emotions had brought them to the present moment. Dennis hoped that maybe this dinner invitation signified that Kay was pulling herself out of whatever rotten mood she had been in for the last year, when they were supposed to be living in newly wedded bliss.

She had been working late a lot more recently, which he supposed could make him a bit cross too. When they were home together, all they seemed to do was argue. *A stressful job could certainly do that to a person,* Dennis thought as he rushed home to change his shirt before meeting Kay. He wanted to look his best for her.

Despite the heavy rain pounding down on his car, Dennis whistled on the way home and into the little shot gun style house they rented just outside downtown Fort Worth. His cheerful tune died in his throat as he took in the fact that the ever present stockings Kay usually had draped over the bathtub were gone and all her clutter of cosmetics had been cleared from the dresser top. An unsettling thought began to form in his mind. Dennis opened the dresser drawers one by one, his anger and disbelief growing as he found each drawer empty.

Who did Kay think she was walking away from him like this? How could she have so calmly and politely called him at work to make her request? At their favorite spot, one of the most significant places in their relationship no less. She might as well have jammed the knife in his chest after pulling the dagger out of his back.

He would meet her for dinner and let her know just what he thought about the matter and her too while he was at it. His mind churning, Dennis grabbed his old military issued rain slicker and slammed the front door behind him. He looked up at the gray sky, prematurely darkened by the thick thunderheads. The wind whipped Dennis's tie into the air with a snap. He was in no mood to be out in the weather being what it was, but he bet Kay had not expected him to go home before meeting her. He was sadistically curious about why she had chosen to meet him face to face rather than just leave him high and dry.

Lightning chased Dennis into Frank's Diner. Carl greeted him from the lunch counter. "Looks like a real gully washer out there. Ms. Kay is over there waiting for you." Carl nodded toward the back booth.

A slight bit of relief coursed through Dennis. *Not our booth.* Even Kay had not been that cruel.

She peeked up at Dennis as he sat down. No warmth shone in her blue eyes or beaming smile played on her lips. Kay pretended to peruse the menu a minute longer. She had never used the menu in any of the times they had eaten there together. Was she using the ruse to gather her words to use as ammunition?

"I stopped by the house after work," he said, baiting Kay to finish what she had started.

"Look, Dennis, don't make this harder than it is," Kay replied in a flat, sarcastic tone. "You know we aren't good together. All we do is fight. I won't take it anymore. I have a job all lined up in Houston. I came here tonight to tell you that when my lawyer sends you the paperwork, you better sign it right away. No messing around or funny business, or Ted will have you served in court."

"Ted! Former boyfriend Ted, who barely passed the bar? Is he your lawyer?" Dennis taunted. Dennis's pulse begin to throb at his temples. His temper built like the fury of the storm outside. Angry torrents of rain beat against the window as Dennis poured out his frustration. He didn't even care that other patrons at surrounding tables were beginning to notice their argument over the racket of the thunderstorm.

Abruptly, she stood. *Kay could never stand people pitying her or giving her anything but adoration.* The cynical thought wound its way through his mind.

"My ride is here. You will get the papers, and you better sign them and be quick about it," she demanded. She shrugged into her rain jacket and grabbed her purse, then quickly dashed out the door.

Dennis stared after Kay. That was it? No fanfare—just apathy and the end of a fifteen month relationship all in less than twenty minutes.

Over the rain, a shrill scream rent the air. Next, came a loud thud. Then a thunderous crash sounded from outside.

Like the other diner patrons, Dennis rushed to the big windows trying to see what happened. The hazy glow of the streetlamp illuminated the street below, revealing a car that was smashed against one of the trees that lined the sidewalk.

A man in a sopping wet bus driver uniform burst through the diner's door. "Somebody better call an ambulance! The driver of the car couldn't see around my bus and hit a lady who ran out into the street." The bus driver turned and dashed back out into the deluge.

Everyone in the diner sat in stunned silence for five, ten seconds. Then like a light switch flipping, words, many words exploded out, zinging this way and that through the air.

"You okay, pal? What about that lady you were with?"

Dennis gaped at the man beside him. Kay had run out that door. His Kay. Dennis was on his feet, moving toward the door with the other curious onlookers. *I have to find Kay.* The rain and the fog from so many hot breaths against the window made it hard to see clearly. Then, as if someone turned a great faucet handle, the rain began to slow to a light patter. Some of the patrons pushed their way outside while others went back to their meals.

Siren shrills rent the air as Dennis stepped out into the cool drizzle. Passengers from the bus were gathered around the upended car with the deep dent in its bumper from the tree that ended its drive. Murmurs began to fill his ears. "That lady surely is a goner." "No way there is anything they can do for her." "The driver is conscious now. Couldn't see around the bus, hit her head on." "Who in their right mind runs out in front of a bus in a rainstorm no less?"

This accident was the scene of a ghastly nightmare; one Dennis desperately wished to wake from. Dennis scanned the crowd beginning to form despite the rain. He skirted the throng and peered at the cars parked along the opposite side of the street. They were all empty save one where a woman sat, appearing dazed while a police officer talked to her. Dennis heard her reply that the victim was crossing the street to catch a ride with her. He paused, relieved that he did not recognize this woman.

The rain and scant lighting was making it hard to find Kay. *Where is she?* He searched the area, hoping to spot her soon. She would be horrified to have witnessed such a tragedy. His mind refused to entertain any other option. It could not have been Kay who was hit. She was his lucky star; life always had a way of working out in her favor. Someone else must be the victim. He would locate her in the crowd soon. Their eyes would meet and all would be forgiven. Tonight, they would go home and hold each other close, grateful for another chance to make things work out.

Finally, he drew closer to the scene in the middle of the road, hoping to be able to make out more of the faces in the waning light. He saw that the woman from the wrecked car had been drawn out and was sobbing against an officer. He did not know her. That was a good sign. Dennis continued to search the sea of rain-soaked faces. His eyes bounced everywhere but at the limp form surrounded by medical workers.

A man in a police uniform jogged up to Dennis. "Sir, were you with a Kay Oswald tonight?" He nodded. "I need you to come with me," the officer said in a tight-lipped manner although his face revealed nothing else. Dennis followed, his steps weighted like lead though he urged his feet to move faster.

Just to the side of the smashed car's bumper the rescue aide workers began to lower a woman who was beautiful and yet badly broken onto a metal liter. The type Dennis had carried in Korea.

Terror and disbelief zinged through his brain. It was Kay on the stretcher. She looked pale and motionless in the moonlight. A large gash split one side of her forehead. Her brilliant blonde hair was matted with blood. *Lots of blood.* Dennis thought he would be sick. He could hear sobbing around him.

The officer who brought him over said, "Sir, I understand this is your wife."

"Yes, sir." Dennis swallowed deeply, knowing he would not like the words to follow.

"She's gone, Mr. Oswald. I am so sorry. There is nothing we can do for her now." The officer looked at Dennis with sorrow-filled eyes and clapped him on the shoulder.

Dennis was dizzy and nauseated. Pitch black darkness began to narrow his vision field. Searing hot then extreme cold were all he knew as bile and vomit spewed out onto the street beside him. He stumbled to the right, then felt more hands tugging him gently. Someone helped him sit on the damp pavement of the sidewalk. Moisture seeped through the seat of his pants but it didn't matter.

Nothing felt right anymore.

Chapter 3

Same Day

Tremors—violent, uncontrollable shockwaves—were all her numb mind registered. The rain that had betrayed her vision and caused her tires to slide, though she braked hard the moment her brain computed movement, had finally ebbed to a light mist.

Most of the onlookers had gone when the ambulance left for the hospital. A prerequisite, the police had explained, although the outcome would remain the same: DOA, dead on arrival. The term had been murmured through the crowd twenty minutes ago.

"Miss?" Pressure and a throbbing sensation pulsed behind her temples as she shifted her swollen eyes up to the bus driver, his hand outstretched with a mug of coffee ready to hand to her. Christine took the cup for something to do rather than out of thirst. Maybe the hot liquid would soothe the burning lump in her throat.

"Thank you." Good manners and rote told her to say. All her brain could do was fall back on what had long been instilled, nothing more.

"There was nothin' you could have done, Miss. I know it. These police boys know it. I suspect your mind will come to know it too one day."

The driver said it with such kindness Christine could cry. She willed herself to hold her tears in check. If one were to fall, ten thousand would join and she would have no hope to keep on.

They lapsed into silence then. His presence was a strength and comfort to hold on to in this madness. Minutes continued to pass by but were not inventoried. Distant church bells clanged seven strokes. The cycle of numbness then frantic tremors were all Christine knew as she sat on the bus stop bench.

"Christine, I will need you to come with me to the station. We will file an official report there," Officer Calvin Simms said gently. Calvin, who had played sandlot ball games and ran high school track with her older brother, who sang tenor in the church choir, and had a bright-eyed boy who sat in her Sunday school class each week, gave her the directive that brought more upheaval to her already shattered world. His eyes were full of compassion as he helped her up from the bus stop bench.

"You will ride over to the station with my partner and I. An officer will bring your car later, if it is able to be driven."

Christine bobbed her head meekly in agreement. She had never even stolen penny candy, but here she found herself in the back of a police car. The lump in her throat began to burn again. This time, no coffee would be offered to pacify it, not that mere liquid could anyway. She had taken a life tonight. Accidentally, but nonetheless, everything had changed in that moment.

The ride was short in distance, yet felt like a lifetime to Christine. She stared out the police car window, seeing her town in a whole new light, one where things were unjust and tattered.

"Would you like to call someone?" the reception officer at the station desk inquired.

Christine fumbled to gather her thoughts. Her father; he always knew what to do. Soon, the operator connected her line.

"Hello, Hinkle residence." The bubbly voice of her youngest sister crossed the wire. That burning sensation roared down Christine's throat once more.

"Hello? Hello!" Her sister trilled in the silence.

Voice as thick as tar, Christine managed, "Alice, get Dad, please, get Dad."

"Christine? Are you okay? What's wrong with your voice?"

"Please, get Dad. Please."

"Okay, just a minute." Soft footsteps pattered away from the telephone. Could eternity happen in a minute? It seemed so tonight.

Dad's voice came over the line, "Christine, honey, what's going on?"

Words. Directions. Paperwork. Trust. She could repeat her testimony to the officers at the station and to Victor, a lawyer friend Dad had picked up on his way to the station. She could sign the stack of paperwork. Dad said she could trust Victor to watch the proceedings carefully and explain what she did not understand. He would ensure that every detail had been handled correctly. The officers were formally releasing her with no charges. Still, they asked her not to leave town until the full investigation was concluded.

At a late hour, when most of the citizens of Fort Worth were tucked safely in their beds, Christine and her father made their way to the home where she grew up. Dad pulled the old family station wagon into the driveway and parked. Neither he nor Christine moved to get out. Their eyes met in the dim lighting. Sobs instigated the tremors that led to the shockwaves. Through it all, Dad held her tightly.

At one point, Christine felt her mother's arms bracing up one side while Dad held the other and guided Christine into the living room. Low voices spoke in the kitchen. Christine was too tired to join them. Instead, she made her way to her old twin bed in the room she had once shared with her sisters. Alice was absent, for which Christine was grateful. How could she tell the younger sister who looked up to her that she was responsible for the death of another human? It was surreal. A woman, not much older than herself had breathed her last breath on earth due to Christine's actions or inactions tonight.

She put her head against the pillow and wept. She attempted to muffle her deep sorrowful sobs with the pillow but could not control anything anymore with the rate the tears were coming.

For the countless time, heavy, swollen eyelids slit open to check the bedside clock that was lit dimly from the street lamp just outside the window. Half past two the arms pointed out. The family dog, Harry, had come in the room with Christine earlier. He was a sympathetic creature who curled up beside her and tried to lick away the tears from her cheeks. However, even Harry had a breaking point. He had hopped off the bed and went to settle in the corner. His light snores echoed through the still room. Christine registered each one of them, counting them like sheep and willing her fatigued mind to rest.

Then came four o'clock; some say it is the darkest hour, though Christine's had been early in the evening. On and on the night stretched before her weary but fretful mind. At six a.m., Christine gave up pretense and made her way by memory through the still dark house to the kitchen. She tiptoed silently down the hall, past the living room, where Alice slept, having given up her long-awaited room of her own, so Christine could have some privacy.

Soon Mom slipped in to prepare breakfast. Christine was at the kitchen table staring out the little window over the sink, watching the dawn break. Her mind was muddled and couldn't string more than a thought or two together. She longed for the days when her mother had carefully guided her through what to do.

Her mother met her eyes. "How can I help?" she questioned softly.

Pain—deep, scorching pain singed her, despite her mother's kind intentions. *If only someone could truly help.* "Oh, Mom, what did I do? What am I going to do?"

"First, let's call Dr. Evans. He will understand needing a day off."

By ten o'clock that morning, five phone calls and a few casseroles had made their way to the Hinkle residence. Christine had stayed in the back bedroom, unsure whether she wanted to see others or be seen by them. The doorbell rang again as Christine finished pinning back her hair with the help of the hall mirror. Mom checked through the peephole and tried to paste a genuine smile on her face before opening the door.

"Mrs. Wharton, I presume. Welcome." Mom greeted her pleasantly, though there was an undercurrent of caution in her tone.

Surprised, Christine looked over quickly, scanning the space behind Mrs. Wharton for Bryan. Christine had asked her father to call the club, or the Wharton residence, if they had left the club, with a message that she had been unable to make it to dinner that evening. Christine had hoped the call would spur Bryan on to call and discover the reason for her absence. She had wondered if he had worried when she was late or if it had given him another cause to be irritated with her. Bryan had not telephoned in the hours since the accident, but the time had grown late, Christine thought, excusing him for the lack of attention. Surely, he would contact her this morning. Perhaps his mother came bearing a message from him.

As her mother and Mrs. Wharton stood side by side, Christine realized that in the year and a half of Bryan and Christine seeing each other, neither of their families had met. She and Bryan dined at the club and went to social events with his family, but it rarely crossed her mind that he would join her family for a change. He had never seemed to expect it.

Sapphire blue eyes set in a strong, elegant face regarded Christine with an edge of something she did not want to put a name to. Mrs. Wharton's expression revealed nothing as she said, "Mrs. Hinkle, I do wonder if I might speak to your daughter alone for a few minutes." Her tone was part Southern sugar, part steel, as if she were the lady of the house with the right to dictate what the following minutes would hold instead of an uninvited guest.

Mom peered at Christine's face for a moment before replying graciously, "I will be in the kitchen making coffee, or tea if preferred."

"There is no need. I will be on my way soon and have much to do today," came Mrs. Wharton's sharp response.

Christine offered Mrs. Wharton their good wingback chair and then sat on the ochre living room sofa. Mrs. Wharton declined the seat and continued her appraisal of the room. For the first time, Christine observed her home as an outsider might. Not one piece of furniture, or the cream-colored walls decorated with family portraits and mementos, or the sweet bric-a-brac collections could compare to the splendor housed in the Wharton mansion.

Once Mom passed through the swinging door to the kitchen, Mrs. Wharton addressed Christine in a strident tone.

"Ms. Hinkle, you know that Bryan is and has always been an exemplary son of this city. He is a peer chosen leader from one of Fort Worth's finest families. He was valedictorian of his high school class, Suma Cum Laude at the University of Texas, second graduate in his class at Yale Law, and is the youngest partner at Fuller, Reed, and Wharton. He is destined for the State House someday. His whole life has been in preparation of the position, and he has kept a sterling reputation." She glanced down her nose at Christine, as she often did when they were near her friends at the club.

Heat coursed through Christine's body. She had a feeling where the conversation was heading next.

"Ms. Hinkle, I have been informed of your culpability in the mortifying incident that occurred last evening." The harsh, accusing statement suspended in the air between them, sucking all the life from the room.

It was an unfair, humiliating accusation but Christine knew better than to interrupt Mrs. Wharton even though she had paused. Having been the recipient of more than one of Mrs. Wharton's dressing downs, Christine could tell Bryan's mother was gearing up for the severe lecture that was sure to come. Christine was too tired, too emotionally spent, to scrounge up the courage or strength to do anything but let the tidal wave of Mrs. Wharton's disapproval hit her with its full tsunami force. Like the furious intensity of the previous night's storm, a deluge of angry, condemning words pelted Christine's tender heart, piercing with their potent message of Christine's failure and her inadequacy to measure up to the glorious Wharton reputation.

Mrs. Wharton finished her tirade with, "Let Bryan go. Do not attempt to hold onto him, expecting our name to save you from your disgrace. If you foolishly demand he align himself with you, you will ruin his reputation and chance to impact this great community because of your selfishness. Is that what you want?"

Mom burst from the kitchen just then, her eyes blazing. Christine had never seen her look so shocked and livid. "It's time that you leave, Mrs. Wharton." Mom's tone was one that Christine had heard addressing an errant, defiant child, but never another adult.

Mrs. Wharton eyed Mom coolly, refusing to acknowledge that her power held no sway in this household. Finally, with a petulant twist of her heel and a huff, Mrs. Wharton stormed out of the house.

Mom slowly sank down to the couch next to Christine. Minutes ticked by on the mantle clock. At last Mom spoke, "You were brave and respectful to a woman who knows how a lady should behave and acted quite willfully the opposite. You could have defended yourself, my darling. You have done nothing wrong. No one could have stopped in time. Your Dad has spoken with the police again. It was unavoidable. They have found no fault in your actions, and they are not charging you with any wrong-doing."

Christine longed to believe her mother's words. They were offered as a balm to her bruised spirit, but Mrs. Wharton's barrage of "You are not good enough for him" and "You do not know how to exist in proper society" rang in Christine's ears like a bell swinging side to side in its tower, each bong clanging, repeating the claims of her inadequacy over her already aching soul.

Later that morning, Meg called long distance from Austin. "Momma told me what happened. Stewart had to go to Corpus Christi this week, so I can't make it up to Fort Worth, but I am praying. You call me if you need to talk, and don't let anyone make you feel bad. Anyone who knows you, Christine, knows you would have stopped if you could have."

Christine managed some sort of thank you before hanging shiny black receiver back on the hallway telephone. *Meg means well. They all do.* Then, she went to answer the knock at the front door.

Carol Ann and Michael, Christine's sister-in-law and nephew, came for lunch and to visit, Carol Ann said. Sweet, energetic, one year old Michael giggled and shoved wooden blocks into his mouth. He had become rather daring, stretching out a drool-covered hand to reach from one piece of furniture to the next. Michael's antics lightened Christine's spirit, breaking through the fog of despair that threatened to overwhelm her.

Before supper, Patty and Margaret, a friend and the dental assistant at Bedford and Evans, stopped by. The three of them sat on the back patio and ate slices of the buttermilk pie one of the church ladies brought over. Gossip about their favorite motion picture stars was the topic of choice.

Christine was grateful her friends were trying to cheer her up and support her. She could tell that each family member and friend was avoiding discussion of the accident or Bryan Wharton. When they thought her attention elsewhere, they studied her, exchanging worried expressions. Christine had caught every one of them in the act a time or two already.

Later, her cousin, Michelle, who came with her mother from Dallas to visit, finally let the cat out of the bag with, "Where is Bryan? Is he working on a big case? I thought I would see him here. It's after six o'clock after all."

Mom was mid-handoff of Aunt Noreen's coffee cup. Her hand trembled at the remark, but with amazing calm, she explained that Bryan planned to visit soon.

Did he? It had been twenty-four hours since the accident, and it was getting late in the day. Christine thought that Bryan would have at least sent a message through his secretary, Mrs. Bronson, if he could not come himself. Bryan had always followed correct social protocol, just as his mother reiterated this morning.

Aunt Noreen and Michelle left as dusk claimed the day's last gleams of light and Dr. Evans thoughtfully told Christine to take the rest of the week off. With no real reason to leave, Christine did not feel like going to her apartment and had already told Patty earlier that she may stay at her parents' for a few days to get her bearings. Many of her high school clothes were stored in the closet of her brothers' old room that had been converted into her mother's sewing room. She had a fresh change of clothes for a few days, and at least there were more people around at home. Although Patty and Christine had faced some tough challenges during their long friendship and Christine knew her friend would rise to the challenge, she could not expect poor Patty to deal with her brokenness on her own. Staying with her parents seemed like the best way to process her churning emotions. They had walked five children through adolescence and were well seasoned in facing adversity.

They were a comfort, though she could tell each worked to give Christine her own time and space. After Aunt Noreen and Michelle drove away, Alice went to her room to study for a history test. Dad was outside weeding Mom's flowerbeds and puttering around the garage while Mom ironed his work shirts and slacks in the kitchen.

As Christine rested in the living room, an encouraging feeling of warmth crept in as she remembered many similar nights from childhood. Of course, back then her brothers, James and Phillip, and older sister, Elizabeth, would all be jostling and teasing one another as they worked through nightly chores and homework or listened to their favorite radio programs. At times, it seemed overwhelming to have so many siblings, but now Christine longed for the security and reassurance being part of a group brought her. Never before had she felt so singled out and alone.

In theory, Christine knew her family and friends were right alongside her, but she alone bore the burden for taking Kay Oswald's life. She alone had taken Dennis Oswald's future full of happiness and destroyed it, leaving him to pick up the shards of his life. She longed for a chance to apologize to Dennis. Christine also wished for the hundredth time she would have seen Kay in time, before it was too late to stop. Almost as an involuntary reaction, she had jerked the steering wheel to the right after hitting Kay Oswald. Her car had slammed into the trunk of a tree planted alongside the street, fortunately stopping its forward motion. Whether it was from the trauma of hitting Kay or the impact of striking the tree, she was unsure, but the last thing she remembered was shifting the gear to park and then she had fainted. Two passengers from the bus had helped her out of her car when she was conscious again.

The wails of sirens had echoed off the surrounding buildings, as rescue aid workers and the police arrived. Minutes later, she had been standing off to the side being checked for injuries by an aide worker when she saw Calvin —Officer Sims—approach a good-looking man who appeared to be in his mid-twenties. Even in the dim lighting, she could see the man turn pale, vomit, and stumble before Calvin and another man from the crowd of onlookers lowered him to the curb. The names Dennis and Kay Oswald had circled through the crowd who kept glancing over at her, some with disdainful expressions and others full of compassion. Christine had been most undone by those caring eyes that spanned the distance, longing to give peace and assurance when there was none to be had. She had destroyed not one but two lives, well, three if she counted her own. In that moment, like no time in her past,

Christine felt that her life was forever different than before and there was no way to go back to the way things were.

"Christine," Dad was at the back door, calling her out of her memories.

Christine left the comfort of the living room to see what her father needed. At the door, she made out Bryan's face in the porch light behind her dad.

"A walk would be nice." Bryan's statement hung in the air for a few seconds. The tone was light but the words were all wrong. Bryan was Mister Efficient. "Never walk when you can drive," he had often joked to the acquaintances he talked with at social events. His sister had laughingly said Bryan's Cadillac El Dorado was the leading lady in his life. Christine had chuckled along with the group while silently agreeing it was so, despite her best efforts.

She grabbed one of her mom's sweaters from the hall closet and followed Bryan into the cool evening air that was common for a March evening in north Texas.

They strolled down the block past the Meyers' house and a few more neighbors before Bryan grasped Christine's elbow, stopping her near the corner, but just out of the street lamp's yellow glow. His eyes flicked toward the nearest porch. Their scan must have brought him relief about something. Possibly, because it was empty of people. With his mother's visit and the way he, who never twirled his fingers or shifted his feet continuously, was doing both as if it would keep him afloat from drowning, Christine knew. This was no casual visit to check on her welfare.

"Christine, do you remember the night of the charity dance where we met?"

The question surprised her. Of course, she did. It had been like floating through a dreamland. She found herself gazing at the most handsome man in attendance and thought for a minute that he had looked her way a few times too. It was fanciful thinking, but she did not have much else to do at the moment. Subtly, Christine continued to watch him walk around couples dancing or chatting on the periphery of the ballroom floor, briefly shaking hands with people along the way. Christine was shocked when he came directly toward her and introduced himself. Bryan Wharton. She had not recognized the name but then again this was not her regular crowd of people. Bryan spent the rest of the evening twirling her around the dance floor and asking her dozens of questions about herself. He was a terrific dancer, and it felt wonderful to have an attractive gentleman take interest in her. The night was as unforgettable as her own birthday.

Bryan continued, "That night you shared that you had little interest in politics or politicking in general. At the time, I thought it refreshing. Mother and her friends had been relentlessly introducing me to women who were not shy about their aspirations to become a politician's wife."

He hesitated; a guilty look filled the brilliant blue eyes Christine's friends regularly referred to as "striking" and "dreamy."

"I think, now, especially now, you deserve to be happy. Have things the way you want them. I have not told you yet, but I have already made inquiries about running for city council. I know it is not the life you dream of." The words whooshed out of Bryan's mouth in a nervous gust, uncommon for his trial lawyer composure.

Bryan continued to fiddle with his cuff link, his eyes fixed on a distant point instead of Christine. He waited. Another skill he had learned as a lawyer.

Christine swallowed, hurt threatening to swell her throat until breath felt no longer possible. Tears burned the back of her eyelids, promising to fall again for the countless time in this nightmarish past twenty-four hours. She had to know though. Make him say it so there was no misunderstanding between them. Christine grabbed Bryan's still turning hand in hers, pressing his palm softly until his eyes had no choice but to acknowledge hers.

"What do you intend?" Christine croaked.

He dropped her hand quickly then and shifted his feet a few times before, "I think it is best if we no longer see one another. We have different goals and dreams." He trailed off. "Let me walk you home," he said in a detached voice.

In the recesses of her mind, Christine had sensed this day would come. His mother's visit this morning had been a warning. Though his argument was flimsy at best, Christine would not beg nor would she plead with him to change his mind. If he could so easily toss her to the side, he was not the man for her. Maybe he had never been, regardless of what she had hoped. As he said, their priorities had always been on other ends of the spectrum.

Summoning what little dignity he had not stripped away, Christine replied, "No, thank you." And turned and walked with measured steps back to the refuge of her parents' home.

Chapter 4

Thursday

The graveside service had been sparsely attended and miserable. The morning had turned muggy with the threat of rain showers in the distance. Kay's mother, Jolene, had come and spent much of her time speaking with some back page, two bit reporter who was hoping to stir up readers by publishing a sob story.

Jolene had wailed loudly throughout the reverend's short eulogy. The gracious pastor had even stopped a time or two so the scant crowd could hear his whole message without interruption.

"You springing for lunch? It's typical for the family to provide a luncheon," Jolene threw at him when most of the mourners, including his and Kay's bosses, had gone.

Dennis and Jolene had never been close. It sure beat him why she would want to have lunch with him. Maybe a free meal was just enticing enough. All he wanted to do was to go home and be alone.

"Sure, what did you have in mind?" he found himself agreeing somehow.

"Just a minute… Timmy. You and Berta, don't leave now. Dennis is taking us to lunch."

Dennis bit his tongue to keep a groan from escaping. These additional guests would be a strain on his pocket book as well as his wits.

Lunch had been a loud, tumultuous affair. Tim and Berta's four kids spilled water, poured the entire contents of the salt shaker out onto the floor, stood on top of the chairs, and screamed so constantly that the family dining at the next table asked to be moved to the other side of the restaurant mid-meal.

Now, back at their—his—house, Dennis did not know what to do with himself. He slung his limp tie across the chair before dropping down on the sofa. His boss, Mr. Mackenzie, told him not to return until Monday. The bank gave three days of paid bereavement. A modern policy, Mr. Mackenzie had said. Dennis had nodded and thanked him.

That first night Dennis felt hot all over one minute but the next, he had shaken like he had a cold. He could not bear to sleep in their bed, so he had curled up on the too-short sofa the last three nights. Each morning, he woke with a crick in his neck and aches all over his body. However, as his muscles stretched and moved, they quickly recovered, all except for his heart. It was sore and aching, and Dennis did not know how to work through its pain.

He briefly considered calling the funeral home to ask how to contact the kind pastor who led Kay's service. The man had been recommended by the funeral director due to Dennis and Kay not attending a church of their own. On Wednesday, the pastor had made a special visit to Dennis's house to discuss what Dennis would like him to say at the service. Dennis had liked the friendly, compassionate man but his name had slipped from his overwrought mind. Today, he supposed that after burying his wife that morning, he was not in the mood for deep discussions. Maybe the pastor could not give him the assurance he needed that Kay would be okay in the end. Could be the pastor would want to know how Kay came to be rushing away from him in the middle of a blinding rainstorm. Would he ask why Kay was leaving Dennis? Would he condemn Dennis for being such an abysmal husband that his wife felt the need to flee him? Would he place the blame of Kay's death at Dennis's feet although he had neither forced Kay to leave the diner nor had he driven the car that caused her body to be struck and then land on the pavement so hard that it had shattered her skull?

Dennis felt pressure mount, roaring through his head, then his heart. It expanded in his chest, pushing his breath and organs to the side. The pressure continued to build through the hours. Rage and despair warred within him, tightening him like a coil he could not unwind. It took up space in his body and mind and pushed him to the edge of his sanity.

Questions with no answers or that could be solved by only the one who could no longer answer churned through Dennis's mind. Why did Kay always want more than he could give? How could she expect so much from one man? Why did she turn and leave him instead of following through with the vows she had so convincingly repeated at their wedding?

Dennis's dad had turned to the bottle when life got hard—beating his wife and kids senseless and leaving scars they would carry in their souls. Dennis swore that would never be his fate. Everything was falling apart, but he would not let alcohol take him farther than he was willing to go. If he could not numb the pain, he had to do something about the mounting heaviness or he would knock a hole in the wall of this lousy, little rent house. Another cost he could not afford when the hospital and burial fees had already dipped deeply into their meager savings.

The dark thoughts continued to brew as he heard a knock at the door. Dennis thought about ignoring whoever it was, but what more did he have to lose by answering it?

Dennis opened the screen door to see a craggy looking old woman not an inch over five feet by his estimation.

"Yes?" He questioned, trying to keep his tone friendly. After all, it was not her fault she chose today of all days to knock on his door.

"I'm your neighbor, Myrna Davis, son. Heard what happened to your wife, and I'm right sorry. I brought you a pie. Berry filling and crust don't make up for the tough blows you've been dealt, but it will fortify you for the battle." Her steady, strong voice belied her size and apparent age. "Why don't you come out on the porch and eat a slice with me?" she invited him.

Dennis was touched by the gesture. At the funeral, Kay's friends and a few coworkers from their jobs had all been kind when they shared their condolences, but no one had offered to come sit with him. He did not know many of them well. They might have felt like they were overstepping or assumed that he had family to bear him up during such a difficult time. Still, the offer might have been nice, though he would most likely have refused it. Could be why he had jumped at Jolene's suggestion to have lunch together. He wanted, even needed, someone to walk with him though this terrible time. He did not want to live it all on his own.

The tantalizing smell of fresh baked pie wafted into his nostrils as he indicated for the old woman to take the lone chair that had been left on the porch by a previous tenant. He leaned against the porch column to the side of her and eyed the pie once more. It sure smelled good. Pie was a rare treat, even though they had enough money for him to indulge in a piece at the diner every once in a while. Kay never made pie for him. He was not sure she knew how to bake much of anything. Sweets had also been a rarity in the Oswald home growing up since all their extra cash and more went to feeding his father's addiction instead of his children's bellies. Dennis loved a taste of berry pie more than just about anything.

Standing out on his front stoop with Myrna, Dennis discovered he liked the old woman, and so did quite a few neighbors based on how many smiled and waved in passing. He and Myrna exchanged minor details about themselves and Myrna shared basic information about the neighborhood and the neighbors that surrounded their houses. After a bit of time had passed, she left the rest of the pie with him and gently told Dennis, "I have known great loss and heartbreak. I have also experienced immense peace and joy. When you are ready to talk about either, I am mere steps away and you are welcome anytime. I'll be back for my pie dish or you can leave it on my doorstep if you would like." With that, Myrna shuffled across the lawn toward her house, which was a nearly identical version of his own shot gun style home.

Turning back inside, Dennis felt the inner fire had cooled for now, and his mood was a bit lighter than before. He might even be able to sleep tonight without taking a stomach tablet or three.

By Friday morning, Dennis had already folded and put away all the laundry for the coming week and picked up the papers and dishes that cluttered the small rooms. He tried to sit and read, but the book could have been a best seller and he would not know the difference for all that the words muddled together on the page. A framed snapshot, one that Kay's coworkers had taken of them at the celebration dinner some of her friends had thrown shortly after their wedding, stared at him accusingly from the end table.

Marrying so last minute at the Justice of the Peace had meant they had no official wedding portrait. In the beginning, Kay talked about hiring one of the stock photographers she knew from Montgomery Ward to take their portrait, but they never got around to it and then the enthusiasm was gone.

They had drifted so far from those first glorious months. He had not recognized the shift until they had chipped away so much at each other that fragments of their hearts were all that remained. They began letting each other's little personality quirks irritate instead of overlooking it as they had done while dating. Dennis was not naturally a contentious person; in fact, he did what he could to avoid confrontation unless it was necessary. Over time, it somehow began to feel necessary to fight. She complained about their lack of finances. He shot back that they made good money but needed to use it more wisely. In the early months, they would argue but ultimately make up quickly; until they each unknowingly stopped. It had become increasingly common for one or both of them to go to bed sullen. Their good times became further and further apart.

Dennis assumed all couples hit a rough patch or twenty in their marriage. He had no experience with healthy marriages because his parents' had been a disaster. Kay's dad had died when she and Tim were young, so she had little firsthand knowledge about how to make a life together. Beside her mom's brief marriage to her stepdad, Larry, whom Kay loathed to talk about, Kay was just as much in the dark as Dennis.

Dennis's stomach groaned, snapping him out of his unhappy visit down memory lane. Yesterday, he was glad he always insisted on keeping at least one unopened box in the cupboard. The saltines brought him a few meals and reprieve before facing the world outside his home. Breakfast this morning had consisted of the last of the pie from Myrna and the crackers. After another quick search, he realized there was no other food left in the house. They had never been ones to keep a large supply at home, because Kay preferred to eat at the lunch counter and pick up supper or dine out most nights. It had been another point of controversy, but Dennis had not enjoyed his own measly cooking enough to force the issue. He figured that should change now that he was on his own again. It would be like his bachelor days when all he could afford was to eat at home. Thankfully, this time his meal budget was large enough to cover more than crackers and apples. He would just have to learn how to fix a few decent meals. Dennis walked the couple of blocks down to the five and dime store, Mott's.

On his way back, Dennis was a few houses away when he spotted an unfamiliar car parked by the curb in front of his house. He shifted the grocery sacks as he tried to make sense of the scene. A young woman, her back turned, put a large suitcase and smaller bag on the porch, then faced the street. Recognition stirred his mind. He had seen the woman at the funeral service. She was with several others whom Dennis recognized as fellow coworkers of Kay's from Montgomery Ward. Dennis knew most of the women, and of those he did not, none of them were recognizable, with the exception of this particular one who had stood at the back of the group. Dennis had puzzled through it later that evening. She had been the driver of the car that Kay was all fired up to get across the street to that night. The woman had stood in the crowd of horrified onlookers as the police asked questions and took statements. She had never said a word to him.

Presently, as he approached the stoop, he read a culpable expression on her thickly made up face. "I don't want no trouble," her country drawl thickly twanged. "These are Kay's personal affects. She stowed them in the trunk after work that day. Thought you might want them. Anyways, I got to get." She gestured to the old Packard. At his nod, she hurried toward it.

The large canvas suitcase and petite vanity case waited for Dennis on the worn wooden porch. This must be where all Kay's clothing and personal items had gone. Dennis had already went through the house. All that Kay left were the pictures of them in better times, the little knick knacks he'd bought her or that she had coaxed out of him, and pretty much any reminder of what their life together had been. By this morning, he had figured that the clothing was gone for good.

Dennis sank to the porch step and rested his head in his hands. *No one stayed.*

It really burned him up. Kay knew how his mother had walked out on his family when he was fourteen. Mom, too, had packed all her valued, worldly possessions and been last seen at the train station. Dennis's mind wandered the wretched path of memories of his father's fits of rage and his mother's crumpled form broken from the beatings. He did not blame her for leaving the unbearable situation but had agonized more than once as to why she had left her children to stay in it. Miles, his oldest brother, made sure the younger kids were fed and got to school until he was drafted to fight on the battlefields of France. He joined thousands of America's sons in their watery graves at Normandy, just months after shipping out.

By the time Dennis made it home from Korea, his sister and youngest brother were gone too. Janet had headed to California in search of work. She wrote to Dennis at Christmas and on his birthday. Terry had run with a mean crowd and was currently serving time in prison for armed robbery and resisting arrest.

A light pressure squeezed his shoulder, drawing him back to the sun's bright light and the buzz of traffic whizzing down the street. "Dennis." Myrna's voice was soft.

He flushed, embarrassed to be found starring off into space while his groceries wilted in the humidity.

"Would you like to join me for lunch? Unless you're going somewhere." She glanced at the two cases that had been shoved to the side.

As if the words alone compelled it, his stomach rumbled noisily. Myrna smiled, and he found his lips turn up a slight bit at the ends. "I guess my stomach would not forgive me if I said no. Let me just put these groceries up, and I will be right over."

Chapter 5

Late Spring and Summer

For the first few weeks following the accident, Christine had not been able to look at her newly repaired automobile without bile inching its way up her throat. Each time she laid eyes on the shiny new hood and bumper, Christine's vision saw only the dent from the tree and the smear of Kay's lipstick that had managed to withstand the rain somehow. The nightmarish images of the accident still filled her head, though the frequency and intensity was lessening. She managed to get almost five consecutive hours of sleep these days. It was only in those last few hours when the mind is somewhere between sleep and waking, that she often jolted awake in a panic from feeling the impact all over again. Rainy nights were the worst. She used to enjoy waking up to the cozy sound of rain pattering on the roof. It had made her want to burrow deeper under the covers and enjoy the steady, peaceful beat of the drops. Now, it triggered her anxiety and fears.

The thought of sitting behind the wheel and being out on the road terrified Christine. Would she accidentally hit someone else? What if a person came near the road and she panicked and hit them as a result? The weight of responsibility ate at her. There was no way to prepare or predict the myriads of scenarios that could be encountered when behind the wheel.

In seconds, her grim thoughts could spiral out of the careful control she constantly sought to maintain. Darkness and despair waged war, seeking to defeat and destroy; to rob her of all common sense and sound logic. All Christine could manage some days was to don her cheeriest smile and keep going through the motions. Could be that no one was truly fooled by her façade, but she continued on because to do any different was to lose the little power over her sanity that she had left. And so, her daylight hours were filled with playing the part of perky Christine who was always fine and dandy, and her nights were consumed by terrors and tremors.

Today, Christine was excited to watch baby Michael while Carol Ann went to a doctor appointment. She had the whole day off from work because Dr. Evans and Dr. Bedford were attending a dentistry conference in Dallas, and she had agreed to spend the afternoon playing with Michael.

The telephone rang and Christine hurried to the hallway to answer it. Mother was at the high school preparing for the commencement ceremony with the other PTA members. She was calling to ask if Christine could check whether she had a few supplies or not.

Suddenly, Michael's piercing wail sounded the alarm that something was wrong. Christine dropped the telephone receiver and dashed to the kitchen where she found Michael's head bleeding profusely. She scooped him up and began applying light pressure with a dish rag. The coppery smell of blood curdled her stomach, but Christine knew that she must tamp down any emotion and concentrate on helping Michael. She carried Michael's sobbing form to the phone, grabbed the receiver, and asked her mother what to do.

"Call Doctor Jensen's office. See what they advise you to do. I will wrap things up here and be home as soon as possible. Make sure to leave a note for Carol Ann," Mom said in the firm but loving manner she had used when instructing her children throughout childhood.

Christine called the office and the staff told her how to quickly bandage the boy and bring him in. She carried Michael to the car as efficiently and gently as possible. She had not driven in over a month but little Michael needed her help. She took a deep breath and calmly backed out of the driveway. Slowly, with sweating palms tightly gripping the steering wheel, she drove the seven blocks to the clinic. There Dr. Jensen and his staff gave Michael three stitches and a lollypop. Michael charmed the whole office, and it was on that air of victory that Christine took him back to her parents' house.

Mom had arrived home to meet Carol Ann and explain the situation. Being the understanding, gracious soul that she was, Carol Ann thanked Christine for her bravery in putting Michael's needs before her fear of driving. Christine worried that Carol Ann would not trust her to watch Michael again, but her sweet sister-in-law reminded her that it could have happened to anyone and reassured her that she had done the right thing with the situation she had been given.

After that, Christine began driving again, mostly for practicality purposes. She knew her parents could not drive her to and from work every day for the rest of her life, and she had proven to herself that she could safely transport a toddler. It was time to start facing her fears.

Eight weeks had passed since her life had been irrevocably changed, and little by little, Christine was feeling like herself again. A week earlier, she had finally summoned up the courage to leave the protective cocoon her parents' home provided and move back to the apartment with Patty. It had been a big step, almost like the first time Christine had moved out of the house two years ago. Patty was grateful to have Christine around again. They had stayed up late talking several nights after work. Already, they were falling into a routine of sharing chores and space once more. The independence allowed Christine to feel capable and in control. She would never forget the accident, but the crushing weight was more of a boulder instead of a whole mountainside.

Today was a truly lovely May day in Texas—Christine's favorite kind of day. The sun was warm, but a cool breeze swelled the air every so often, keeping things pleasant. Big, blue Texas sky stretched as far as the eye could see with not even a single puffy, white cloud for miles. At work this afternoon, she and Margaret opened the small window of the reception desk area. Almost everyone who entered seemed buoyed by the lightness of the spring weather.

Only Mrs. Livingston had commented on how an open window might give people a chill or invite in unwanted insects. They thanked her for her consideration but neither moved to address the critique, which would be one of many before she left the office, based on past experience.

Christine headed over to the large filing cabinet by the window and stretched her neck to let the cool gust blowing in seep around her collar. It was her favorite spot for a peek at the world outside the four walls. As she filed patient records, Christine heard her name float across the breeze.

"That girl has never taken my requests seriously. Apparently, she doesn't take much seriously. I saw her laughing with Margaret Dooley. You would think she could act more remorseful for what she has done. A young woman has left this world forever because of her." Mrs. Livingston's caustic words were directed to Mrs. Locke, who would be walking in for her two thirty appointment in just minutes.

Christine had known about the whispers and gossip concerning her part in the accident. She had seen heads bent close together part quickly when she was noticed. During Christine's first trip to Mott's after the accident, she had watched three neighbor boys peep around the aisles giving her the side eye. She had heard one boy say, "That's her. You better watch out when crossing the street." The soles of the boys' shoes practically slid as they rushed to round the corner onto another aisle. Had it been just two months earlier, Christine would have laughed at their over dramatic, almost comical attempts to avoid her after her identity was confirmed.

However, Mrs. Livingston's gossip was more painful. She was in the same social circle as Christine's recently passed grandmother. A community of women who had congratulated Christine on losing her front teeth, watched her learn to ride a bicycle, and chaperoned her first dance. Christine had always pictured herself becoming like them when she grew older; instead, she faced the censor and disdain of a prominent member. The cruelty, the injustice of those words, threatened to break the levee Christine had carefully constructed to hold in the raging of her soul.

The bell at the office entrance jingled. Christine turned away quickly and wiped the tears at the corners of her eyes. Then, she pasted on her cheeriest smile, hoping it would be convincing enough. "Good afternoon, Mrs. Locke," she greeted.

Mrs. Locke approached the desk and blanched when she detected the open window. Margaret gave Christine a concerned glance over her shoulder when she came to take Mrs. Locke back for her teeth cleaning.

Christine sighed after Mrs. Locke left for the exam room. *How can I move forward if others won't let me forget what I have done?*

At the end of the week, Christine joined her parents and Alice as they drove to Dallas to help with cousin Michelle's preparations for her Saturday afternoon wedding. Christine was a bundle of nerves. Mrs. Livingston's gossip had intensified her anxiety toward the upcoming weekend events. It would be the first time most of her aunts, uncles, and cousins had seen her since before the accident. Christine was not sure how much further reproach she could withstand from people who claimed to care about her.

How would they react? Would her family and friends act kindly to her face and then turn around and speak poorly of her? Uncle Dale had never been one to hold back his thoughts on any topic. Michelle's brother Johnny was also known to forsake other's feelings if he had an opinion on something. Thankfully, her parents would be around for much of the time. People were less likely to talk badly if close family was present.

All day Friday, the cousins decorated the church with sashes of ribbons, greenery, and large silk bows at the end of the church pews. They also arranged fashionable, waterfall style, bouquets of white orchids and gardenias complemented by sprigs of pink bouvardia to add color. The bridesmaids would carry the lovely spray of flowers and the groomsmen would have a simple white orchid pinned to their lapel. Christine was relieved when the young women's conversations remained centered on Michelle, her groom, her wedding gown, and their wedding trip to a romantic retreat in the Smoky Mountains of Tennessee. Michelle giggled and blushed, happily soaking up the attention.

That evening, Christine sat in the church pew observing the reverend direct the bride and groom, their attendants, and their parents through the ceremony rehearsal. Christine fought the urge to let her thoughts drift to Bryan. Her heart was still so tender and wounded from how he had treated her. His abandonment in her worst hours had been a cruel betrayal. It reminded her of the time in her childhood when she stepped on a sand burr while running barefoot through the grass. Though her mother had pulled the burr out, part of the sticker remained, burrowed deep, irritating the painful injury for days after.

"Hello, mind if I join you?" her cousin Steve asked. At Christine's assenting nod, Steve slid into the pew beside her. Steve was the son of her Aunt Veronica, Mom and Aunt Noreen's other sister. He had always been Christine's favorite cousin because he was generous in spirit and had the best sense of humor of anyone she knew. He would pay a compliment often and could coax a smile from their angry mommas even when they had tracked mud onto the kitchen floor. Steve would grin at them until his joy was shared by all.

"How are you doing?" Steve whispered. He met and held her eyes with his own. "Be honest."

Truth. Christine could not keep from being truthful with him. Not only because he was her favorite cousin. He had fought in Korea. He knew the deep, irreversible sorrow of having taken a life.

She thought for a moment, wanting to get the words right. "I feel as if I have broken something sacred and precious and there is no paste or remedy that can ever restore it."

Steve listened and waited. The compassion and empathy in his expression never wavered. It urged Christine to share her true feelings.

"How…how did you stay so happy despite…" Christine hesitated, "despite the war, the killing." Never before had Christine felt the right or even had the desire to ask Steve such a probing, personal question.

Steve looked at her thoughtfully, knowingly. As if their brains both questioned, "How can I heal, move forward when the one I hurt can no longer do the same?"

"The Lord, he is the only hope in this life. His daily grace gave me the ability to live out each hard day and let me tell you, there have been some difficult ones."

Christine sighed. "I know the church answer, Steve, and I'm trying. I do pray. It just seems that I should fix things too, for the husband. I certainly cannot bring her back…" Though Christine did not complete the thought, Steve understood.

"Keep trusting him, Christine. Focus on Christ's character. When you know him deeply, it changes how you experience and handle everything in life." Steve smiled and tipped his head toward the front of the sanctuary where they were being signaled it was time for the rehearsal dinner.

Thunder clapped overhead and a heavy rain began to pound down on the roof. For the rest of the evening and on Michelle's wedding day, the thunderheads seemed to have set up camp.

Christine thought the wedding was beautiful despite the rain. Michelle wore an in-vogue tea length gown of ivory satin with delicate gloves. With misty eyes, Christine observed how Michelle had no other focus but her groom as she marched down the long church aisle toward her future husband. Michelle glowed as Glenn raised her veil, gazing at her face with such love and pure joy.

The reception was a simple but lovely affair held in the church fellowship hall. Christine and Elizabeth helped serve punch made from grandma's well loved recipe and an almond vanilla wedding cake baked by Aunt Noreen. The bride and groom dashed from the reception hall to a waiting automobile in a mix of rice and raindrops.

By six o'clock that evening, Dad, Mom, Alice, and Christine piled into the car to head back toward Fort Worth. As they made their way westward, the sun broke through the clouds. Golden, coral, crimson, indigo, and violet splashed across the sky in unique pattern and form. The combination was spectacular. What had been dark and dreary under the cloud to the east was now, with a few miles position change, radiant light and incomparable beauty. The car had gone silent with all of them taking in the majesty. When twilight finally chased the last of the light away, they remained quiet. Each of them seemed content letting the others process the grandeur of what they had seen.

It was meaningful to Christine. In a way, it was an answer to her sorrow-filled prayers. She could stay under the raincloud of despair, letting other people's opinions and actions bombard and weigh her down, or she could choose to change directions, walk out from under judgment and accept the forgiveness she had already been given.

Christine was not naïve; she knew it would be quite the challenge, but she was determined to try, to push out the dark, discouraging thoughts and walk freely in the light of mercy and grace.

Her resolve was tested over and over in the following weeks. She noticed the curious, almost accusing look a neighbor sent her when she hummed happily as she helped weed her Mom's flowerbed. More obvious were the twitters and pointed fingers of some of Alice's classmates while Christine enjoyed a milkshake at the soda fountain on a Saturday afternoon. There was no refuge for her, even at her church, which her family had attended long before she was added to the bunch.

At the end of May, Christine began teaching the Kindergarten boys' Sunday school class once more. The boys were loud and unruly at times, but Christine found their hearts to be sweet and kind as well. She had missed the boys' liveliness and enthusiastic stories in the weeks following the accident but believed it was best to take the time off. Due to the encouragement of the pastor and Ms. Jackie, her own childhood Sunday school teacher, Christine took up the role again.

One Sunday morning after the boys rushed to meet their parents to attend the service, Christine tidied the disheveled classroom quickly in order to make it before the opening hymn. She winced sharply after cutting her finger while gathering the left over craft paper. As paper cuts always do, the sliced skin bled and throbbed in pain. For such a small wound, the injured area pulsed long after the finger was bandaged and she had finished cleaning the room. She would be late to the service, but there was nothing to be done about it besides noiselessly slipping into the back of the sanctuary.

While walking through the deserted halls heading to the sanctuary, Christine heard her name bandied about. She caught several women huddled together as she turned the corner just outside the Sunday school hallway. They quickly broke apart but sent Christine looks of disapproval and scorn. Their unkind manner felt like the paper cut. It rankled her far longer than the brief encounter should have.

Sadly, it was not the first time she had found herself the subject of such ladies' gossip. Christine thought a well-meaning church member must have notified the pastor of the rampant issue because the congregation had already had two consecutive sermons on the repercussions of gossip in the church and compassionately loving your neighbor as yourself. While Christine appreciated her pastor's care, she had felt like sinking down low in the pew throughout the duration of both messages. She had imagined all of the congregants' eyes staring at her, and obviously these women had not taken it to heart.

"Press on," became Christine's mantra. The more she focused on who Christ said she was, the less she carried the burden of living up to how others expected her to behave.

It was difficult in practice but her freedom was the reaped reward.

The scorching days and weeks of summer arrived swiftly in Fort Worth this year. The spring's cloud covered days and rain gave way to temperatures in the upper nineties and low triple digits beneath an unrelenting sun.

With the heat wave came more changes. Nelson Richards, Meg's cousin and their former schoolmate, was back from Ole' Miss.

Nelson had shown up on Patty and Christine's doorstep one evening in mid-May. The girls invited him in to catch up. Though Nelson was eager to talk with both of them, Christine noticed how often he sent covert looks at Patty when she was turned away. She recalled how Nelson had behaved similarly in high school. What she had not put together as a school girl was obvious now that she had gained a bit more knowledge and insight into relationships.

Although Christine had thought him a bit of a nuisance in high school, Nelson really was a nice guy, or maybe he had grown into one. He was smart and genuine. Christine could not recall when her attitude toward him had shifted but thought Patty could certainly do much worse than an intelligent, kind, college graduate with a job and a healthy bank account. At the end of their visit, Christine invited Nelson to come over the following Saturday night. She promised to have a fresh, homemade cake for him, which made Patty's eyebrows rise up near her hairline. Nelson happily agreed. When Saturday evening came, Christine finished frosting the cake right as Nelson arrived. After a bit of chit chat, Christine claimed that she need to take a few items for her mom's Sunday school lesson over to her parents' home, but that they should eat the cake without her. Patty shot Christine a funny look but graciously invited Nelson to sit down at their small dinette table while she sliced a generous serving for Nelson and a smaller portion for herself. Nelson looked ecstatic at the arrangement.

Nelson did not take long convincing Patty to leave her childhood crush behind and see him for the man he had become. Though it came as a slight surprise to Christine, apparently Nelson had been laying the groundwork for some time.

At first, Patty had been cautious to share the news with her. She told Christine she worried the last thing Christine needed was to hear all about how wonderful her life was going. Patty shared that over a long distance phone call, Sheila reminded Patty that her relationship could not and should not be hidden and that Christine had always wanted the best for her. It had prompted Patty to sit Christine down that very next evening to share what had transpired between her and Nelson in the past year and what was happening now.

As Patty told her all that occurred in the past few months, Christine was impressed by Nelson's gumption. She had not figured he had it in him. In the weeks following, Christine realized that in the past she had missed many of Nelson's redeeming qualities and had discounted him too quickly. She was thrilled that he was a man whom her friend could love and respect and who equally admired and esteemed Patty. Still, Nelson shocked them further when he proposed a few weeks later. He told Patty he loved her and wanted to spend his life with her on July 4th as fireworks boomed above, their sparkling light casting a romantic glow. It seemed that when Nelson finally got up the nerve to take action, the man acted with haste!

Meg, Christine, and Patty's cousin hosted a bridal shower in early August. Meg drove into town a few days before to help with the hostess duties and spend quality time with her friends. Patty, Christine, and Meg sat up half the night before the shower, giggling as Meg revealed all of her cousin's secret thoughts about Patty throughout the years and as Patty retold the story of their whirlwind courtship.

Christine had sighed, contentedly listening to how in the ninth grade Nelson swore Meg to secrecy after she overheard him tell his mother he wanted to invite Patty to the fall homecoming dance. Meg also recounted several times when Nelson lamented to her about how he got jittery around Patty and could never say the right thing. He had worried that Patty only viewed him as an obnoxious, privileged kid who knew little outside of the world of cotillion and country clubs. His concerns had been warranted. By the end of their junior year at Ole' Miss, Meg advised Nelson to stop talking about the missteps and misused time at home from school and directed him to do something to change the problems. She had married Stewart earlier that fall and had watched the way Nelson moped about the reception anytime another man asked Patty to dance.

Together, they concocted a plan for Nelson to prove his sustenance and avoid acting like the schoolboy Patty overlooked. Last autumn, Nelson wrote Patty a short note ending in a question. Patty was puzzled to receive the letter and had not even mentioned it to Christine because she was unsure why he had written to her since they were never close friends. Nevertheless, she answered it to be kind to an old schoolmate. Her answer had given Nelson hope. In the following months, a few more letters were exchanged. Patty and Nelson were to have met for lunch during Nelson's winter break from college but Patty had taken sick with bronchitis. Patty had ended up in the hospital for a few days before being released to recuperate at her parents' home. Christine recalled seeing a large vase full of yellow roses, Patty's favorite flowers, but had never asked who sent the flowers that had adorned Patty's childhood dresser that week. Meg shared that Nelson had called her in despair over Patty's condition and wondering what he could do, or if Patty had a favorite flower. The flowers had been Nelson's doing. He was patiently, steadily paving his way to claiming Patty's heart.

Patty told Christine and Meg she had been waiting to interact with Nelson in person again before she could be sure that he was the man from his letters instead of the obnoxious boy of their youth. When the accident happened, Christine missed the signs of the blooming friendship that was becoming more than one-sided adoration. Nelson had graduated from Ole' Miss in early May and made his way home a week later. He had accepted a job at Leonard's department store downtown, and now he wanted to get the girl too.

Now, it was August, and they would marry in three weeks. Neither Patty nor Nelson had wanted a long engagement. Their mothers had immediately begun calling venues as soon as the proposal was accepted. It had been miraculous that there were openings at both the church and ballroom. Nelson declared it was a sign of blessing from above, and so they rushed to send out the invitations, find dresses for the bride and her attendants, and order the cake.

Even with the main details planned, Patty was a-flutter. Bridal magazine clippings covered every inch of their small dinette table. Lists of all kinds could be found on the sofa end tables. Christine did not mind the clutter. It was refreshing to focus on living instead of being so caught up in macabre things that could not be changed.

One evening, Patty and Nelson came in to the apartment with peaked expressions on their faces. "Christine," Nelson said after Patty nudged his hand. "Today, Bryan's response card arrived. He is bringing a date to the wedding."

Patty had warned Christine that Nelson's parents had been obligated to invite the Whartons. The families attended the same church and throughout the years both patriarchs had sat on several boards together. While Mrs. Richards was compassionate toward Christine, she was not one to shirk social obligations.

Christine nodded. She held back the tears that sprang to her eyes.

The wedding would be the first time Christine saw Bryan since the night he ended their relationship. As she helped Patty address invitations, Christine knew she would have to prepare herself if Bryan did indeed attend. Now that she learned he was attending and with a date no less, Christine wrestled the feelings of inadequacy and heartache surging through her thoughts, threatening to overwhelm her and tear away her hard-won peace. *Press on,* she charged herself once again. There would be sorrow and inner storms, but she must keep pressing on because she wanted to experience the good times that were surely on the path ahead.

Chapter 6

Summer 1955

In the months following Kay's death, Dennis found himself vacillating between anger and remorse. Kay's suitcase and valise had sat in a corner of the living room for three weeks before Dennis could bring himself to move them. It was insane of him to think that by leaving the bags out, the whole nightmare would somehow be erased and Kay would waltz through the door saying she ought to put the old things away.

Crazy as the idea sounded, a little part of Dennis dreamed it was true. Day after day, there the cases sat. While readying himself for work, Dennis passed by them, avoiding the silly things, as if that would resolve everything. At night, while he read on the couch to wind down and relax, he turned his body to face the opposite wall from the cases.

There was no one around to notice the dust that began to gather on and around the bags. Dennis and Kay had rarely entertained at their home. Kay claimed that having people over was too much of a bother and that it was better to go out to meet friends. Dennis had agreed, lest he end up cleaning the whole house himself or listen to Kay rant while they picked up and straightened the clutter together.

Once Dennis finally moved the cases into the bedroom, the bags spent another week unacknowledged until Dennis stubbed his toes on his way to the bathroom late one sleepless night. The following day, the suitcases waited like unwanted strays hanging around, begging to be accepted. No matter how difficult the task was, Dennis promised himself he would tackle sorting through their contents that evening.

Without Kay, he had fallen into his former bachelor routine. He left for work at 7:30 each morning, lunch was around noon, and the work day ended promptly at 5:00 p.m. He came home and heated up a can of soup or beans or ate bread and butter. Some nights, Dennis went over to Myrna's house. She had become an odd sort of friend, but he realized that he enjoyed her company. Myrna fed him nutritious, warm meals with meat and vegetables. Usually, there was some type of sweet treat afterward. In an unspoken exchange, Dennis addressed items in disrepair around her home and tried his hand at fixing them. They had a good laugh when the kitchen sink pipe got clogged and Dennis was sprayed in the face while disconnecting it. He was no handyman but had learned a few tricks out of necessity throughout his years. Myrna seemed grateful for the help and his company too.

Although work and Myrna filled some of his waking hours, Dennis spent much of his time after five o'clock alone. The suitcases had waited in these lonely hours. It was not just Dennis wanting to avoid the memories that made him pause. Kay had been very insistent on her privacy. Though he had owned the chest of drawers before they married, after the blessed event, Dennis was assigned three drawers in their dresser. Kay was adamant that he leave her drawers alone. If she bothered to put her wash away, it was done when Dennis was out of sight. She rarely kept anything too personal out in the open. "It's just how I was raised," she had told him when he tried to help her during the first month they were married. Only knick knacks, makeup, and perfume bottles cluttered the top of the dresser. There was a lot of that sort, so Dennis could not imagine how messy things could have been if she kept all her items out.

It was now seven o'clock that evening; Dennis had eaten supper, cleaned the dishes, and prepared his lunch for the following day. There were no other pressing chores that needed to be done. Dennis dragged the bags back into the living room and in front of his favorite chair. He figured he might as well get comfortable for the inevitable journey into his greatest and worst memories.

He stared at the cases for a bit, as if opening them would make him a traitor to Kay for unlocking her bags without permission. Finally, he worked up the nerve to turn the locks.

When the case sprung open, he inhaled the cloying odor of Kay's favorite perfume, Femme de Rochas. The scent had not been his preference, so Kay had not worn it much since their dating days, until that last month. He remembered being irked at Kay because she put it on a time or two or came from work with the fragrance on her clothing. He thought she was wearing it to get revenge due to their latest argument. Perhaps it had been a warning that something significant had shifted between them.

Dennis began to pull out the meager contents of the cases. A few dresses, undergarments, and sweaters lined the inside. Not the full extent of Kay's wardrobe, which had been yet another source of contention between them. Dennis's anger still flared when thinking back to their numerous arguments concerning how much of her pay went right back to her employer, Montgomery Ward.

During one particularly heated argument last January, Dennis had angrily shouted, "New hats, shoes, party dresses, day dresses, and jewelry. When will it be enough? We have bills to pay." Kay had snottily informed him that it was part of her job to look her best. She claimed Ward's customers expected the employees to wear higher quality clothing or they would not feel confident in buying from the store. He'd tried to appeal to her sensibility with, "We could live in a nicer neighborhood if more money came home each month." She had told him that it was his job to provide for the housing and her income was merely a supplement to cover minor living expenses. Dennis had been so angry, he hastily left the house and ended up walking coatless in the near freezing weather. When he'd arrived home again, he was chilled to the bone but the bedroom door was locked and Dennis had spent the night on the couch with only the warmth of the coat he had left behind earlier. It was one of many sordid recollections that sprang to mind as Dennis sorted the items. How could things have gone so wrong between them in such a short amount of time?

After surveying the contents of both bags, Dennis figured the woman who brought the cases back must have thought he was too unobservant to notice the missing clothing. Who knows what Kay had told her about him?

Dennis was also disappointed that the only reminder of him that Kay had packed was a gaudy, faux black cat pin he bought her their first Christmas together. That December, while window shopping at Leonard's, they had noticed the little cat pin with striking emerald eyes nestled in a white velvet-lined box. Kay instantly fell in love with the broach, saying it reminded her of a neighbor's cat when she was growing up. She had looked at him with shining eyes, full of childlike excitement. Dennis had loved her for it, and pulled her inside to the counter to buy the expensive piece of jewelry. They had eaten beans and rice for two weeks straight to recoup the cost, but her joy had been worth it.

He decided to give the clothing to Myrna to donate through the program at her church. Dennis laid the pin on the dresser top at first, but what had once brought oohs and ahs now pricked his heart, sending waves of guilt and sorrow coursing through him. He shoved the pin to the back of his sock drawer.

A few days later, Dennis decided to pay Myrna a visit and give her the box of unneeded clothing. He had not seen her in days, preferring to keep his own company and perhaps wallowing in self-pity a bit. Myrna had not been out on her porch as much lately either, most likely due to the searing summer temperatures. Not that inside these houses was much cooler, but some relief was better than none. He had better see if she had a fan. If not, Dennis had a spare that Kay used to move around the house to keep cool on days like these.

After Dennis knocked, he heard, "Let me just see who that is." Myrna must have a guest. Dennis did not want to intrude. He planned to hand her the box and head home.

"Dennis, wonderful to see you! You bring that box back to the kitchen and come meet my friend." She glanced at the box inquisitively. When they walked into the kitchen, Dennis noticed a diminutive, young man sitting at the table munching away on a generous sized cookie, occasionally stopping to dip it into a glass of milk.

"Leon, this is Dennis, my friend and next door neighbor," Myrna introduced.

Dennis studied the man. His blond hair was combed and his clothes were pressed and tidy. He appeared to be younger than Dennis by a few years. He had almost a childlike innocence to him as ate the sweet treat.

"Dennis, meet my friend Leon. We attend church together." The younger man nodded with a shy smile. "Leon lives on the next block over and has come to visit while his sister picks up a shift at the diner." Frank's. Myrna did not specify which diner, but it was the only café within walking distance of the neighborhood.

When Kay was alive, Frank's used to be dinner a few nights a week. These days, Dennis could not bring himself to walk or drive past the place. The idea of eating there again made him nauseous.

In truth, he went out of his way to avoid the whole block vicinity surrounding his once favorite place. He shuddered, remembering Kay's blank, unseeing eyes and ashen face, looking up at him from street level. He doubted he could walk around there again without envisioning her blood splattered on the pavement, intermingling with the rain water and forming rivulets of red that washed the street anything but clean.

"Would you like to try one of my maple pecan short-bread cookies?" Myrna said it with her back turned, giving Dennis a moment to catch his bearings.

"Yum, yes, more cookies, please," burbled Leon happily. The first words he had spoken.

Myrna looked at Leon fondly, handing him another large cookie. "This young man loves my maple pecan cookies. I make them special when I know he'll be by for a visit."

Dennis knew Myrna did not have much room in her budget for extra expenses. Though she appeared to have all that she needed, he could tell that she did without and sacrificed so she could give to others. Her generous spirit amazed him.

The three of them chewed happily on their cookies. The scene was so ordinary; Dennis was struck by the drastic turn his life had taken. A few months ago he never would have pictured himself in such a gathering. Dennis and Kay went dancing at night clubs, out to the movies, or to dinner with their friends. Mostly Kay's friends; she had drawn a crowd while he had been a loner with one or two close friends. Sure, he had made a buddy or two during his school days, and had been on friendly-enough terms with Jerry, Dusty, and Craig while their roommate. He even had a couple of guys he palled around with during his stint in the Army, but none of them lived nearby anymore and were not the type to correspond. At the bank, he was always friendly to the other employees but primarily kept his head in the books and got his work done. His father lived less than four miles away, if he was current on his rent, but Dennis wanted no part with the man who had knocked him senseless on more than one occasion. The sad truth was Dennis could not currently claim a single true friend of his own beside the woman at whose kitchen he sat, and possibly now Leon, if one was being generous.

Dennis could never figure what brought him back to Fort Worth after his time in Korea. Maybe it was familiarity because it certainly was not the fellowship of family or friends. Might be, he had gotten as caught up in the dream of home as the other soldiers who actually had loving families and friends to return to. All the same, here he was, in a humble kitchen—one where he knew he was wanted. Dennis soaked in that warm feeling a moment longer. "I had best be getting back home." Hopefully, he said it with enough conviction to make them believe he had a lot more to do than sit around by himself until his mind could wind down enough to rest.

Myrna dipped her head in acknowledgement, then grabbed his hand and held it between her own wrinkled ones. "Thank you for the clothes, Dennis. It was very kind of you. These clothes will go to the clothes pantry to help several ladies throughout the year."

"I wish…" Dennis wished many things: that Kay had not died, that she had not been leaving him but had stayed or at least given him a fighting chance to change her mind. "I wish there was more," he opted to finish in place of pouring out his voided yearnings.

Leon reached out and patted Dennis's shoulder, astonishing him. He had forgotten the quiet man was in the kitchen. "Good bye, mister. You be okay." Leon's slow drawl echoed through Dennis's mind later that night.

Would he be okay? What did okay even mean? All his life, Dennis had been on a tough road. An angry, drunk of a father with a third grade education, a mother who left her kids behind to fend for themselves when she could not take any more physical abuse, a brother who was buried in foreign soil, and now a dead wife. When would he be okay?

Mary Arnold

Dennis knew the other man was no seer of the future, but he grasped on to the hope that someone thought he would be okay.

Chapter 7

Late August 1955

Fragrant arrangements of gladiolas and long-stemmed roses sat in elegant crystal vases on all the reception tables, and beautiful silk ribbons bedecked each guest's chair. Decadent chandeliers dripping with crystals lit the enormous ballroom, giving it an intimate atmosphere. While Nelson and Patty's church ceremony had been simple and sacred, the reception was all luxury and sophistication.

Christine sat at the table reserved for the bridal party and did her best to steer her eyes away from the opposite corner of the dance floor where Bryan expertly led a tall, graceful woman in a waltz. Bryan's date wore a gorgeous, pale blue gown that was encrusted with large, sparkling diamonds. From an outward appearance, the only thing Christine had in common with the woman was the dark brunette coif of their hair. Otherwise, they differed in every way. It could be that this new woman had a sweet disposition and was known for her kindness to all. Christine worked hard to keep her thoughts gracious and enjoy her friends' special day. She was thrilled for Patty and Nelson. That must be her focus for tonight.

Meg watched her and smiled encouragingly. "Stewart, take Christine out to dance." She blushed prettily and patted her slightly mounded stomach. "This baby is still making me feel queasy when I move too much, but y'all should enjoy a dance for me." It was a kind but feeble attempt. Sheila walked over then, saving Stewart the trouble.

"Hey, y'all," Sheila greeted them. Her bouffant hairstyle was Texas-sized, as was her signature confident attitude. In the years since high school, Christine and Sheila had exchanged letters, had a few long distance phone conversations, and visited each other during Sheila's occasional trips to her childhood home town. Sheila had written double the letters in the past few months, assuring Christine that she was supported and heard in the midst of the difficult days. It meant so much to Christine for Sheila to spend precious minutes away from studying for her final examinations and lab research to care for a friend. It was even better to have her here in person. The night before, Sheila and Meg had both spent the night at Patty and Christine's apartment. They all stayed up talking late into the night until Meg played the mother role and sternly told them they would regret the lack of sleep when there were bags under their eyes in the morning. That got Patty ushering them all to bed real quick!

Sheila tugged on the sleeve of a tall, good-looking man that had come to the table with her. "Y'all remember Pete Ashby? I found him over by the punch bowl and told him it was time for a reunion," Sheila said, followed by a loud laugh.

Pete smiled and greeted Meg and Christine and shook hands with Stewart. Stewart asked Pete about his job. Christine's mind drifted back to what she remembered about Pete because she had not seen him since graduation. In high school, he was the go getter type. He was the class president one year and Student Body president their senior year. Always working toward something, similar to Sheila. They were often competitors and complimented each other well. Christine was curious about what he had done with his life over the past four years. Sheila went to church with him growing up and had been assigned as his pen pal through a church program meant to encourage their boys overseas, but had not mentioned him much in her letters to Christine. For all her bluster and gregarious nature, Sheila could be tightlipped when she wanted to be. Maybe Pete was one of those things she wanted to keep to herself.

Breaking into Christine's musings, Sheila leaned in and whispered, "He sure grew up well, didn't he? He works for the city's public works department as an electrician and volunteers in the community." Pride in his accomplishments was evident in her tone.

Sheila pulled away and addressed the group in a louder voice. "That reminds me, Pete. You said in your letters that you are looking for someone with office skills to train your students. Christine has a business school degree and manages a dentist office here in Fort Worth. Y'all should talk about her volunteering with your program. She might be the right fit for what you are needing." Pete smiled the same infectious grin Christine recalled from their school days.

"Christine, I would like to share my program's mission and needs with you. If you are up for a dance, we can talk at the same time," he said earnestly. Pete looked at Christine, his expression both encouraging her to join him but giving her the freedom to decline if she wished.

Christine agreed with a smile and accepted the hand he held out. Belatedly, she turned her head back, almost seeking Sheila's permission, but the outgoing woman had already launched into an enthusiastic retelling of some childhood memory.

Pete led Christine to the dance floor and twirled her before settling down to sway softly to the band's version of Nat King Cole's popular song "Unforgettable" and to share his "mission" as he promised.

Pete explained that he had found himself with too little funding to attend college after graduation. Soon after school let out, he began working for a friend of his father who was an electrician. When he was drafted for service in Korea, the Army used his electrical knowledge and skills and gave him more training. In Korea, he had been struck by the numerous amounts of people both abroad and from back home who lacked the basic training to work in skilled jobs. Several of the guys in his unit had subsisted on next to nothing before they joined the Army. Pete promised himself that when he hit U.S. soil, he would do what he could to help those in his community learn useful skills so they could obtain better jobs.

After speaking with the pastor at his church and presenting his idea to the congregation, a job skills program was created with help from his father and a few other church members. The program was less than a year old, but already the instructors had noted that many of their regular attendees were showing improved understanding of concepts and learning marketable skills.

"Right now, we are meeting on Tuesday nights in the fellowship hall of my church, but I hope to have a building of our own one day. We allow anyone to be trained through our classes and sometimes that bothers certain community members. I don't want the church to suffer because a few hotheads can't understand that God wants good things for all His people," he explained.

What a kind and meaningful concept! Christine was impressed with Pete's program.

"Please think on whether you would want to teach typing, filing, or any office skill you think is valuable to know. Christine, you could make a real impact on someone's life." Pete's enthusiasm was contagious.

"I will," she found herself agreeing while taking the small card with the program's information on it from him and placing it in her purse.

Meg waved her over. "They are going to cut the cake soon. You may want to fix your makeup and hair before your maid of honor toast."

Christine agreed and went to freshen up in the powder room. She had just finished straightening her panty hose in the bathroom stall when Mrs. Wharton's voice sounded across the room from the mirrored vanity.

"Oh, yes, Sylvia. Kathryn does look fabulous with Bryan tonight. They are quite in love, and I would not be surprised if Bryan is inspired by tonight and proposes soon."

"She is clearly a young woman of beauty and good breeding," the nasally voice which must belong to Sylvia replied.

"You know, Sylvia, they were in fact intended to meet in this very ballroom a little under two years ago? Unfortunately, Kathryn had a family emergency at the last minute and was unable to attend the charity event that evening. There was some confusion after that—of course, you know all about that other girl and her despicable incident. Thankfully, they had been introduced this past February. It was just a few weeks afterward that they began seeing one another exclusively. His father would have been so pleased to see him with Kathryn. I certainly am. "

Sylvia sighed as if she had listened to the recitation of an epic love story. "All's well that ends well."

With that, the powder room door opened and closed with a whoosh. Christine leaned against the stall door, stunned. Fragments of the night she and Bryan met floated in her mind's eye. Meg had invited Christine to the charity event and offered any dress in her wardrobe as further incentive. Christine had been able to take the afternoon off and schedule a last minute hair appointment. Later, she had twirled in front of Meg's enormous bedroom mirror, feeling like a princess in the pale mint sequined gown. Meg had grinned and told Christine she would take every man's breath away.

Christine had found herself enjoying the beautiful event, although the only people she knew there were Meg and Nelson, and Stewart. Though Christine was not sure he counted as knowing, since she had only met him for the first time earlier that evening. She and Nelson had laughed and caught up while they danced around the ballroom a few times, but he'd left her at their assigned table to talk with some friends also on break from college.

For a while, Christine had scanned the room captivated by all of the glamorous dresses and room's chic décor. Meg and Stewart had waved as they danced by a few times. Christine was not sure what else one did at these sorts of events, but knew she must keep herself from fiddling with the beading on the handbag also on loan from Meg.

At some point the air had taken on some sort of strange, electrified energy; Christine looked up trying grasp at what had changed. Her eyes came to rest on a very handsome man standing on the edge of the dance floor. His eyes pierced hers across the distance, or so it seemed. She had never seen such a good looking man in her life. She would remember it well, if she had. Christine's jaw had nearly dropped when he appeared to head her way. Then he stopped to shake hands with a group of men. Christine swallowed, disappointed but not surprised. She had taken another sip of her lemonade for lack of something else to do and scanned over the crowded dance floor for the umpteenth time.

"Excuse me, Kathryn?" a smooth baritone said from in front of her. Christine looked up, stunned to see that the suave man from across the room had indeed come to speak to her.

"It's actually Christine," she told him, wishing that she did not have to contradict the first words between each other.

He had nodded but Christine remembered being unable to read his expression. Then he flashed her a perfectly brilliant smile. "I must have the details wrong. I'm Bryan Wharton. It is nice to meet you, Christine."

Christine and Bryan had laughed and talked and danced the rest of the evening. She had practically floated home on the euphoric wave of romance. Meg demanded to know all of the details and filled in a few about Mr. Bryan Wharton, a member of one of Fort Worth's finest families.

Now, in the same bathroom mirror where two years ago Christine had wondered how she, an average girl, had attracted such a catch, she saw a girl with dull, world-weary eyes. The awareness that her meeting Bryan had been the result of a mistake or fluke of some sort, one that had been discussed behind her back, tore at the tender scab covering her still healing heart.

Why had Bryan continued on with their relationship for so long? Surely, his mother informed him of her inferior qualities soon after the switch was realized. What had been the point? Could it have been as he said the night he broke her heart, he had found her refreshing, for a time? Had he ever truly liked her for who she was? Was she a pet project? Maybe she was a chance to endear himself to the working class voter in his community in preparation for a future election. Christine had tried not to hate Bryan after he discarded her like trash when she became a liability to him. Patty, Meg, and Sheila had told Christine countless times that she was better off without him. Unfortunately, their words did not take away the sting of his rejection or the bitterness at being deemed unworthy by someone who had claimed to care.

"Christine, dear?" Mother peered into the powder room looking for her. "Darling, what has happened? Are you all right?" Her face had taken on an anxious, fragile expression Christine had seen frequently this summer. Mom always tried to mask it quickly, but Christine knew the accident had taken a toll on her too. She never burdened Christine about it. Nonetheless, Christine had noticed the way she worried and hovered more than in the past. Things had not been easy for any of the Hinkle family since the accident. She had overheard her parents discussing the way some acquaintances had snubbed her mother or sister in public and how Mom had lost the PTA presidential race though she had served the two previous school terms with tremendous support.

Christine gathered her thoughts, unsure how to put into words all the pieces her mind had pulled together in an attempt to understand the truth. As the ladies' room door swung open again, Meg joined them. "It's time for the speeches…" She trailed off. "Oh Christine, you are pale and your eyes are red. Are you feeling okay?" she murmured, compassion tingeing her voice.

Collectively, Mom and Meg waited. "I learned something tonight, and it upset me, but give me my handbag. I won't let Patty down." Brave words, all fluff and bluff.

Christine didn't want to face any of them. Mrs. Wharton's conversation left her feeling exposed—a laughing stock—like the accident would be all anyone saw about her anymore. It was as if the sum total of goodness Christine had done in her life was stripped away and the label murderer was stamped boldly in its place. No matter that the police had cleared her and found no fault, just an unfortunate chain of events, in her actions. Some people would still see her as not good enough give this speech honoring her friend; to be their friend or marry their sons; to hold a place of leadership' and on the list could go.

She powdered her nose and reapplied a thin layer of lipstick while thinking back to the summer at her grandparents' farm. Christine and her siblings had been asked not to eat blackberries before supper. She and her brothers snuck out and ate dozens of tangy, juicy berries. At supper, they had been asked what they had been occupied with that afternoon. They had lied and made up a big story about playing and swinging from the towering old Sycamore tree at the back of the yard. Grandma then asked why they had lips stained purple and seeds in their teeth. Each of them missed out on blackberry cobbler as punishment for disobeying and lying. The stain on their teeth remained for a day or two, a reminder of what they had done. Would the stain of the accident be forever with her, tainting the way people saw her?

She glanced once more in the mirror, pinched her cheeks, and mustered what courage she had left, "I'll be fine. Let's go."

Christine ascended the stairs onto the small stage after the best man, Nathan, spoke. She shared a brief childhood memory of Patty and herself and then of Patty and Nelson. Christine ended with a toast that their marriage would be blessed with love and goodness all of their days. It was not the speech she had planned, but Christine descended the stage, pleased that her friends had been honored and that she could hold her head high.

The bandleader began playing "Pledging My Love," and as couples filled the dance floor again, the crowd thinned enough for Christine to notice Mrs. Wharton pinning her with a pointed look, a smirk, if one could say a high society woman smirked. Had Mrs. Wharton known Christine was in the ladies room before she and Sylvia entered? It was too cruel to imagine, but the proud gleam in Mrs. Wharton's expression hinted it was truth.

Sheila grabbed Christine and pulled her toward the area where all the unattached young ladies waited for the bouquet toss after the song ended. In the shuffle of making room for more women to join, Christine found herself standing next to Kathryn. She was even lovelier up close, the quintessential Wharton bride. Patty gave the bouquet a respectable toss. Kathryn reached through the air and caught the blissful bundle, a fitting metaphor for Christine's life. All that had seemed fairytale perfect was gone or taken by another.

After seeing Nelson and Patty dash to a limousine waiting to whisk them off on their honeymoon, Christine returned inside the ballroom to begin packing up the gifts. Although there were a good number of guests lingering around and talking, she kept to herself. Her thoughts turned again toward the stinging words she had overheard in the ladies' room. She had not intentionally hit Kay Oswald, but she was paying for it nevertheless. Everywhere Christine turned the path was blocked by the brambles of her failure to avoid hitting Kay, by her lack of money and social status, by her not being enough. Where was the easy path or the straight way that she had enjoyed as a child? The times when Christine made straight A's without studying, got elected to the student council on her reputation alone, or was given an afterschool job because her neighbor had put in a good word for her with the owner. How long would she have to trudge along ostracized and outcast? When would others let her move on with her life instead of relegating her to an eternity of paying for her mistake?

Chapter 8

September 1955

"Dennis, I would like to see you in my office at three o'clock this afternoon." Mr. Harris's tone was friendly, but Dennis anxiously counted the hours down for the rest of the morning. His meager lunch of bread, cheese, and an apple could have tasted like dust and he would not have known.

At five to three, Dennis tidied his desk and walked to Mr. Harris's office. In the two years Dennis had been employed at the bank, he had spoken to the bank president only when greeted each morning and briefly when Mr. Harris came to his desk to convey his condolences about Dennis's loss of Kay.

Dennis hoped the jitters inside his stomach were not noticeable on the outside. Ms. Stanwick, the president's secretary, prompted Dennis to enter through the closed door.

"Dennis, right on time." Mr. Harris looked pleased. He shook Dennis's hand and gestured for him to take a seat in one of the rich cognac colored leather chairs right in front of his desk. Dennis's boss, Mr. Mackenzie, sat in the other chair, and smiled at Dennis. *Hopefully, that was a good sign.*

"I'll get right to the point. We have been impressed by your work ethic and efficiency. Mr. Mackenzie, here, has been singing your praises for a while now. I would like to have you train for a management position. This will mean a department change, but Mackenzie and I think it will be a good fit for the skills you have. What do you say?"

Sweet relief surged through Dennis. He still had a job. In fact, he had a chance at a better job. Dennis had not felt such tremendous reprieve since he landed back on U.S. soil after his time in Korea. These past months his job had become the only constant in his life; Dennis had clung to the routine of going to work and the stability of it. To be frank, work had kept his hours filled and his mind sane.

Dennis gave his assent and Mr. Harris outlined the new position and what his training would be like. Dennis was excited about all that he would be learning and working with and was eager to start the fresh challenge. It was more than he ever expected and imagined. He thought he might have to work at Worthington National Bank for a few more years before an opportunity like this was offered to him.

The day was pleasant reminding Dennis that autumn was on its way. He whistled on his walk home, until it struck him that Kay had been their celebration planner. As soon as she heard the good news, she would have called a fancy restaurant for a reservation. They would have had splurged on a swell dinner; maybe they would have met a few friends for dessert and then gone dancing until their feet ached and the champagne bubbles made them float.

Grief hit Dennis like a strong punch to the gut. He missed Kay. They'd had some really good times together. Dennis had forgotten that in his anger at Kay walking out on him.

Kay had been his golden girl. A light and ethereal beauty in appearance and demeanor, her laughter and carefree attitude had made him forget how hard and cruel the world could be. Dennis regretted not pulling her close for a hug more often. He was ashamed of all the times he failed to reconcile with her after they argued. To his disgrace, he honestly could not recollect telling Kay that he loved her much beyond those first initial months of their marriage.

Dennis swiped at something blocking his vision. Moisture. Tears. His mind whirred seeking to understand what was happening. He, who felt so much shock as he held Kay's icy, lifeless hand at the hospital, had not cried then. Neither had Dennis shed one single drop during Kay's memorial service or in the days following. But here, on one of his happiest days, rivulets of tears trailed down his face, cleansing it and his spirit.

A tingling sensation spread throughout him, almost like when a body sits for too long and when it stands, pain reverberates in the numb limbs, reminding them that they are living. Dennis's spirit had been numb half his lifetime, it seemed. Though these memories of Kay brought pain, it was good to get them out and use them again. It somehow made him feel more human, more alive.

"Sir, are you okay?" a plain young woman asked breaking through his reverie. She was wearing the standard uniform of Frank's Diner employees.

"Swell, thank you." Dennis tipped his hat to her, noticing for the first time that he had stopped walking and appeared to be crying and staring straight into a drab, brown house on a block that he recognized as one too far from his home. He turned back to the lady who gave him a reassuring smile and headed in the direction of Frank's.

Dennis moped around the house all day on Saturday, restlessly moving from room to room unsure what to do. He tried to put away the laundry, but the empty drawers haunted him. He had yet to move a few articles of the clothing from his cramped drawers over to those Kay had once laid claim to. He attempted dusting, but the lack of objects to dust made him despair. Not much was left of Kay. What she had not taken with her, Dennis had removed or packed up and given away in his anger. The tiny house's walls began to press in on him. He wanted to sleep and forget about it all but sleep could only be snatched in small increments. It reminded Dennis of being on active duty in Korea. Only this time, the enemy was not flesh and blood; it was the memories of his mistakes, the image of Kay's unmoving, bloodied form lying on the pavement, and the ever present lure of his old man's demon, alcohol.

Sunday morning dawned, greeting a blurry-eyed Dennis who had managed three hours of sleep. Dennis knew he was a wreck. He imagined he looked terrible because he felt even worse. His head pounded from the lack of sleep and the disturbing, guilty thoughts that seemed to run through his brain continuously.

Around 11:00 a.m., there was a knock at the door. Dennis was sitting on the couch with a cooled cup of coffee debating whether or not to ignore it when the rapping began its steady beat again. The taps were soft but persistent. Dennis figured he might as well answer the door. Leon stood on the threshold looking sharp in his pressed, dove gray suit with a white dress shirt and matching tie. *He must be fresh from church.*

"Myrna, she has lunch ready. She says to come get you," Leon drawled, dutifully extending the invitation.

Dennis glanced down at his pajamas, deliberating inwardly if he should accept the invitation or not. Myrna seemed to care about and accept him as he was. She had become the closest he'd had to a mother in over a decade. He guessed he could put on real clothing and eat with her when she asked.

He told Leon to wait a minute and directed the man to the sofa while he hurried to the bedroom to change. Dennis splashed water on his face but decided that the two day old growth on his chin would have to stay for today. He was more alert now and followed Leon to Myrna's house.

Myrna welcomed Dennis at the front door. "Glad to see you, my boy. I have been watching for you this weekend." She said it in a manner that made him feel cherished and not scolded. In the recent weeks, they had taken to drinking their Saturday morning coffee on the front stoop of her house while shooting the breeze a bit. There was something special about communicating with another human as the sun's first golden rays lit the world around them. It revealed a fresh, new day that was full of possibility. He had not seen it as such until his morning time with Myrna. He and Kay always slept late after a busy Friday night out. Being an early riser naturally, Dennis figured his body had reverted back to old preferences when it no longer stayed out late.

Now, Dennis was ushered to the small, round table in Myrna's kitchen. He smelled the tantalizing aroma of some kind of roasted meat from the stovetop. A dish with mashed potatoes and its twin full of glazed carrots already waited on the table.

"Well, howdy! This sure smells and looks good, Myrna," Dennis said.

Myrna's wrinkled face took on a rosy hue at the praise. "Thank you, son. It's my birthday, and I thought to share it with my loved ones," she replied.

Dennis began to notice the other guests already seated around the table. He recognized Ms. Brenda, Myrna's friend from church who came to sew with her on Tuesdays. Mrs. Railey from further down the block smiled back at him. Dennis also remembered her as his sixth grade History and English teacher. Leon sat on her right, and next to him was the petite young woman whose house he had been caught staring at on Friday afternoon. She observed him with an amused look. He noticed that she had pale green eyes and mousy brown hair. Today, she was wearing a blue floral dress instead of the café uniform.

"This here is Essie Mae. She is Leon's sister and my good friend," Myrna introduced. "I think you know everyone else here." Dennis nodded to her and went to the seat the ladies indicated would be his for the meal. Myrna led them in a simple prayer and began passing the serving dishes around the table.

The next hour was the ideal picture of a home full of love and friendship. The food was every bit as delicious as it had smelled. The company was even better. They all told stories and laughed loudly with one another.

Ms. Brenda had baked a vanilla cinnamon cake in honor of Myrna's birthday. After they sang "Happy Birthday" to her, Myrna shooed the younger three out onto the back stoop with a generous slice of cake on their plates saying that the three old friends would clean up. Leon dug into his piece immediately, sighing appreciatively. Essie Mae nibbled her slice in silence. Dennis wanted to explain why he appeared to be staring into her home the other day, but how did one share such a thing with a stranger?

He tried to read her expression out of the corner of his eye. "I…" he started almost unconsciously. She met his eyes, curious. "I was lost in my thoughts the other day. Didn't mean to scare you. I know it was strange to see a grown man, a stranger no less, crying outside your house." That had to be one of the most awkward things he had ever said to a woman. Not that he considered himself a particularly smooth talker, but he had been good enough to keep Kay's attention, for a while. His cheeks became warm with embarrassment.

Essie Mae assessed him before speaking. "I'm made of stronger stuff than to let that get to me, but thank you all the same." Her soft voice and small frame suggested otherwise, but who was he to say what someone could or could not withstand. In Korea, he had seen big, burly men cry over the loss of a buddy while others shut everyone else around them out and focused on the task at hand.

The quiet between them thickened for a beat or two. Then, "Thank you for playing checkers with Leon. He has been so excited, and has come home jabbering about it a few times. You remind him of our older brother, Louis. Leon misses him and the farm a lot."

Dennis was glad that he had spent the time playing checkers with Leon. Yes, it had entertained him too, but seeing the other man's pleasure at having a willing opponent had made it even more worth it. Dennis watched Leon for a moment. Leon was childlike in his joy at seeing the neighbor's dog bound around its yard. "He's a friend to me too," he replied.

Essie Mae flashed him a sweet smile. "I thank you for that." She paused, then shifted the topic. "Myrna said you were born and raised in Fort Worth. We come from a farm outside of Graham, but have lived here for three years now. Leon needs to be close to a doctor and at times, a hospital, if his seizures come on more regularly. Back home we all watched out for him as best we could, but it got to be too dangerous when the tremors would start. There was no way to get him help quickly, especially one without a long, bumpy car ride. Here, I do my best, and Myrna is a godsend. I cannot be with Leon all the time, but we have a telephone line installed. I taught Leon how to call if he starts feeling bad, and Myrna and our neighbor are able to look in on him throughout the days when he is not at the corner store."

Essie Mae stopped again and took a minute, as if trying to formulate her thoughts before speaking them aloud. "You may have wondered a bit about him and that is all right—many people do. Some ask questions, and Momma made sure we older kids all knew how to answer them with grace. 'Folks are just curious, most not intending harm but wanting to understand,' she would say. Leon was born with a condition some scientists and doctors are calling Down's syndrome. The doctors have told Momma and Daddy it affects his mental abilities, growth, heart, and might be in part the cause of his seizures. There is still a lot of research to be done to understand the condition. We love him all the same. No matter what research and data are discovered, we know that Leon is a gift to our family and has taught each of us so many lessons over the years. What we've found is that Leon is a good listener, and, with a patient teacher, he is able to learn to do many tasks on his own. In fact, a few days a week, he walks down to the five and dime store for an hour or two and gets paid to do chores around the property. Because I am now working shifts at the diner for some extra income, he comes to Myrna's, that way he is not alone so much. Myrna has been a real blessing to us. Being how he is, Leon is kind to all, but needs real, genuine people who call him friend. Your kindness means a lot to him and me."

Dennis absorbed all of the information Essie Mae shared. He was surprised that Essie Mae, who seemed kind but fairly reserved at first meeting, would entrust him with it, but he was glad she had. He had found himself wondering about the siblings during the birthday luncheon. Essie Mae's momma was right. Being willing to share a little about Leon had opened Dennis's mind to a world he had no experience with and helped him understand his new friend better. It inspired Dennis to look for ways that he could include Leon.

After that, they spoke of lighter topics like the weather and the neighborhood for a few minutes longer until Leon indicated that he was tired and wanted to go home for a nap. Dennis followed the Kuntz siblings inside to say good bye and thank Myrna for the fine meal. He kissed the old woman on the cheek and told her how much he appreciated her including him in her birthday celebration. Her smile back related pure joy.

As the shadows grew long, Dennis went back to his lonely house, this time his restless spirit at peace. He felt a satisfied happiness from the time spent in the presence of those who cared about him. Dennis knew that not all problems could be fixed by mere mortals like himself; however, he was grateful that people like Myrna and Ms. Brenda and even Leon and Essie Mae could be part of the healing.

Chapter 9

October 1955

After Patty's wedding, Christine had to move home with her parents, but not for lack of trying to find another roommate. Most of her close friends were married or had moved away from Fort Worth. She had asked around at church and with acquaintances, but no one seemed interested in renting a garage apartment—not with her at least. Christine went as far as placing a classified ad in the local Penny Saver. One gal was interested and met Christine for coffee and to see if their personalities and schedules were a good fit. All seemed to be in place until the following evening when Veronica telephoned and said that her parents would not allow her to live with Christine. Christine worked hard not to be devastated by the occurrence, but the disappointment was an additional strike to her injured spirit. There were no other reputable applicants after Veronica's reply, and so, Christine's independence was another loss due to the stigma from the accident.

Christine felt mortified and humiliated. Each time she was rejected, it stung. Could no one realize that if she could have prevented hitting Kay Oswald, she would have? She was no criminal who purposefully sought to take another's life. Why did people insist on treating her like one? When would her penance be enough for them? Christine made an extra effort to look her best and be helpful when called upon to serve. She tried to make excuses for others' callous behavior toward her. She attempted to forgive them when they hurt her feelings. Christine told her mom as much as they packed her apartment belongings and loaded them into her parents' car.

Mom listened sympathetically, advising Christine to keep living in a right manner and over time people would take notice, or they would get caught up in someone else's scandal and focus on that instead. "I wish that I could take this all away or kiss it better like I did when you scraped your knees as a girl. Christine, I am proud of the grace and perseverance you have displayed throughout this time. I am not sure I would have handled things quite as maturely when I was your age. Though I may not have a solution, I am always here to listen and support you." Mom said. Christine hugged her mom and thanked her.

The first week back at home, Christine enjoyed her mom's pampering and listening to the radio at night with Dad. It was a cozy reminder of her innocent childhood. But nostalgia could not fill the lonely nights for long. Alice was in her senior year at Arlington Heights High School. Christine tried not to feel a bit envious of her. Alice was on the cusp of adulthood, her whole life ahead of her. She flitted from school to her afterschool job shelving books at the library, club meetings, football games, and time with friends. It made Christine miss days gone by when she had a calendar full of fun activities to do and people to spend time with. In high school, Christine would have pitied her present self. Unfortunately, she had no better ideas on how to help her present situation now than she would have then. Mom and Dad would not share their opinions and thoughts on the topic unless Christine directly asked. Christine knew they wanted her to feel in charge of her own future.

So she went through the motions of living. On Sundays, she taught Sunday school and attended church, then prepared for the week ahead. Monday through Friday, she went to work from seven thirty in the morning until four thirty in the afternoon and then came home to read or spend time with her parents. The weekend nights were quiet. Occasionally, she would meet up with Patty but knowing that newlyweds needed lots of time together, she let weeks lapse between visits.

All Christine could do was pray, wait, and use the techniques she was learning to help herself process her guilt and bitterness. She was sure that her mom was correct. Better days were ahead, but how she would get there, Christine did not know.

On the second Tuesday in October, autumn began to show signs of fully joining them, ushering out her over-staying relative, summer. Christine always loved the crisp north Texas mornings and pleasant afternoons, which were highly anticipated and greatly appreciated after the summer's heat. The cooler weather gave Christine the pep she needed to finish sorting through the last of her boxes from the apartment.

Following Mom's prompt serving of supper at 5:00 p.m. when Dad got home from the office, Christine vowed to sort through all the papers until the job was complete. This final box would be particularly difficult. It contained photos and mementos from her months of seeing Bryan. Before Bryan, Christine had been on a few outings and dates. The relationships were rarely anything that lasted long and had ended mutually. Bryan had been her first love, though now, she wondered if she had loved the idea of him more than his actual personality and character. What girl would not be impressed by a man who could afford to bring her roses each time they went out, who lived in a mansion, and who could take her to expensive restaurants and exclusive events and plays? It had been a dazzling, exciting world to her, for a time. Christine had kept the ticket stubs, the pressed flowers, the play bills, and other mementos to commemorate their dates. To get rid of it all was to finally admit that his betrayal had happened and reconciliation would never be possible. Not that she even wanted to go back to the way things had been; it simply felt like the death of a dream.

Christine stared at the box, then willed her hands to pull out the first item. A crimson rose she had pressed from the lavish bouquet Bryan presented to her on their first date. Christine had never been fond of red roses, but the gesture had been romantic. Into the waste bin it went. A mound of playbills and movie tickets came out next, followed by a Star Telegram clipping about Bryan's speech in honor of his late father and his charity endeavors. Then there were a few photographs of her and Bryan. She was surprised to realize that she did not appear truly happy in any of them. Her smile was off. It seemed strained or forced. There was no sense in analyzing why it had been so. They were all trash now, she felt no further need to look at them and remember.

Then Christine fingered a small rectangle of card stock. She almost added the card to the waste basket but glanced at it quickly. She recalled taking it out of the purse she wore to the wedding but had misplaced it in all the bustle of moving. "FREE career skills classes," it read, then listed Tuesdays at 6 p.m. and the address of the church. The card was for Pete Ashby's program that he talked so fervently about at the wedding. She had forgotten about the classes after overhearing Mrs. Wharton and in the hectic packing of boxes to move home.

Her wristwatch read 5:55 p.m. The church was only a few minutes' drive away. Christine grabbed a sweater. Now that the program Pete was so passionate about was on her mind, she had the urgent desire to go and see how she could help. She was not sure how to contact Pete other than through Sheila, and she knew no gal liked the idea of her friend calling up her guy while she was away. Going to the church was the best option, and she would do it tonight before she lost her nerve. She would show up and see if Pete meant it when he assured her she was welcome and there was much work to be done. Christine's parents looked surprised when she rushed into the living room and told them that she was going out to volunteer at the church and didn't know how late she would be getting home.

Christine walked into the church fellowship hall at 6:10 p.m. The large room buzzed with voices and activity. There appeared to be four groups, one at each corner of the room. A group of five people of various ages and backgrounds sat in folding chairs intently watching a teacher who held up different objects and pronounced the name associated with it, the students repeating the word after him. To their left, a woman around her mother's age spoke softly to two mothers holding infants. One mother had two other small children playing quietly on the floor beside her. Next, a group of high school age young men sat at a table with an older man. Thick text-books were spread out all across the table top. The instructor would occasionally ask one of the students to write on the roll out chalkboard behind them. Finally, Christine spotted Pete in the farthest corner from her. He was talking animatedly with another man and typing on a typewriter every so often. When Pete glanced up to survey the room, his eyes landed on her. The large grin on his face made Christine glad she had come. He said something to the young man and joined her by the door.

"Christine, it's good to see you and for you to have come." His warm and inviting smile chased away the worry that Pete would turn her away as others had lately. "Let me introduce you to Mark and get your expert opinion on the résumé he and I have been typing up for him. Later, I will show you more about our program if you are interested in volunteering with us." Pete's words and inclusive attitude bolstered Christine. Someone would let her join them, be a part of their group. It was a simple thing, but Christine no longer took belonging and acceptance for granted.

Mark told her he had completed technical training and an apprenticeship as a plumber. However, his boss had a son joining the family business soon and did not want to pay two employees. Mark had a family at home who was counting on his paycheck, so he needed to find steady employment soon.

Christine's business school classes taught her about creating a professional résumé that was both honest and sure to impress employers. She and Mark discussed his training and experience and formatted a résumé to highlight his strengths and skills. Her fingers flew over the typewriter's keys, and within the hour, Mark had three neatly typed resumes to deliver to potential employers. In the remaining time, they went over best practices while interviewing. Mark left appearing more relaxed than when Christine had met him the hour and a half before.

Pete had stayed with them at first, but after her reassurance that she and Mark were just fine, Pete circulated the room checking in with the other three groups. At 7:40, Pete announced that it was time to pack up for the night. The students chatted as they filed out and said goodbye.

"I'm sorry I didn't make it back to you," Pete apologized. "I got caught up in explaining idioms to our English language students. Let me introduce you to our other volunteers."

Pete called the others over. Two men and a woman gathered around Pete and Christine. "I would like to introduce y'all to a friend of mine, Christine Hinkle. She is a secretary for Bedford and Evans Dentistry, which you may be familiar with. I am hoping to talk her into leading our business and office skills students."

"Christine, please meet Dave Carmichael, Joe Battaglia, and Dolores Peterson. Dave is an English teacher at Heights and teaches our English language learners. Joe is an engineer by day, and he volunteers with our students who are studying for vocational testing. Dolores is a nurse at the newly renamed John Peter Smith hospital, which we grew up calling City-County Hospital. She is teaching health and hygiene to anyone with questions and is our contact for those who wish to learn more about entry level jobs in the medical field. The final member of our team is my Pop, who was not able to come tonight. He prepares students who would like to take the U.S. citizenship test and helps anyone who has questions on filling out employment documents."

Each member of the small group welcomed Christine warmly and expressed how glad they were that she had joined them and that she might take on the time-consuming role of building résumés. The group then set to work restoring the room to order. With the chalkboard clean and rolled into the closet and the tables rearranged, they all walked out into the brisk night air.

Pete warned Christine that it was best to walk out with at least one other volunteer. Occasionally, they would have a visitor or two who wanted to share their displeasure at the program being available for people of any background to participate in. Christine had remembered Pete sharing a similar sentiment when he first told her about the program. Whatever had occurred must have placed Pete on alert, because his face was very serious both times the matter had come up.

With his dark hair, glasses, and plaid shirt, Dave reminded Christine of her father. He piped in, "I don't understand why some people can't let others have something as plain and simple as education without getting bothered by it."

"We may never understand why they protest, but we must persevere in spite of their antics." Dolores spoke with the conviction and authority of a nurse who was used to dealing with all sorts of people. Christine instantly liked the determined older woman who had a trendy flair and exuded energy and a passion for helping others.

Being unfamiliar with the layout of the church, Christine had parked a ways down from the others. Pete walked Christine all the way to her car. "I'm really glad you came. You had Mark's résumé done in a flash." He held up his hands, fingers splayed out. "These fingers are great for using a wrench but clumsy when having to peck at those tiny keys." He smiled. "If you want to talk in depth about the program you can come early next week. I usually arrive around 5:30 to set up, or if you would like, I can stop by your parents' house on Sunday afternoon to discuss details."

"I can come early next week," Christine replied, uncertain if Sheila would be bothered by Pete visiting her at home. It was better to play things safe, especially when she had so few true friends these days.

Pete nodded and waited for Christine to close her door and start the engine. He waved as she backed out and turned the car toward home. Her parents were still reading in the living room when she entered. "How was volunteering?" her mom asked with interest. "What program meets on Tuesday nights? Your father and I could not think of one."

Nearly overflowing with excitement for the program, Christine proudly explained Pete's mission and the classes he and other church members had created to do their part to improve the lives of those in their community. She practically bubbled with joy as she shared how Mark had left looking hopeful and more prepared for his job search. Mom and Dad agreed that it sounded like a wonderful program and encouraged Christine to keep volunteering. They were so inspired that Dad went to search for paper and other supplies to donate for the students' use and Mom promised to collect old books for the students to read and household items that could be made into first aid kits for families.

Christine felt a deep sense of satisfaction for the first time in months. She had helped another improve himself, and she had met people who saw her for who she was, not what she had done.

The subsequent Tuesdays, Christine helped several people create résumés and discussed ideas on how to search for job opportunities with their skill sets. Christine and Pete held mock interviews and worked through any questions the applicants had about the process. Mark had sent a few friends to the program who happily reported that he had successfully obtained a job.

The second week, Pete's dad, John Ashby—also known as Pop—was back and introduced himself with the same enthusiasm as his son. Christine recalled seeing his friendly face in the crowd at high school events years ago. Very quickly, she found that she liked John very much. She could tell that he passed his sense of humor and positive spirit to his son, not to mention that looking at him was like seeing what Pete of the future would be like. They had the same narrow nose, generous smile, and thick chestnut colored hair with hints of copper, though John's was also streaked with gray. It was astonishing how similar the two men appeared both physically and in temperament.

Christine enjoyed bantering and planning with Joe, Dave, Dolores, John, and Pete. Despite their different ages and stages of life, they were becoming her friends. Soon, Christine anticipated Tuesdays more than any day of the week. When she was not at the classes, she spent her free time scouring the newspaper's classified ads for job listings. She was eager to tell her students about the ads and help them prepare to answer the notices.

At the end of October, the whole group celebrated when Paola reported that she had been selected for a highly

sought after position at Leonard's department store. Paola had been one of the program's first students. Dave had taught her English terminology and correct grammar. John helped her study for the U.S. citizenship test. Pete trained her how to complete business paperwork and file, and Christine had assisted with compiling and typing her résumé. The job was a testament that their efforts were making a difference in the community.

On the first Sunday in November, Christine found herself thinking about the program as she took a walk at one of her favorite parks. North Texas could be downright cold by November, or it could be as pleasant as a spring day. Today, a light sweater was perfect for a stroll in the autumn afternoon sun.

Alice had friends over at the house, and Christine had not wanted to interlope on their fun. She decided to use the time to brainstorm a way to provide a proper interview suit for a student in need without wounding his pride. She wanted Willy to make a good impression but not at the expense of embarrassing him. Lost in her own thoughts, Christine did not notice someone calling her name until the man approached her side.

Christine was happy to see the familiar face of Scott, Patty's older brother.

"Christine, good to see you! How are you?" Scott greeted her with a radiant smile and a hug.

Surprise rippled through Christine. This version of Scott was almost unrecognizable. It had been years since she had seen him without dull eyes and a grim set mouth.

Here he stood before her; an older replica of the man Scott was before joining the Army to defend the world against Hitler and Hirohito. The transformation was astonishing.

"I'm well," she replied still trying to grasp how different Scott seemed. "Sorry, I was day dreaming and did not hear you. How are you?"

"Swell! Say, would you come with me? I want to introduce you to someone and catch up a bit if you have a minute. You looked pretty busy at Patty and Nelson's wedding so I never had the chance." At Christine's agreement, Scott led her to a blanket under a tall oak where a woman sat while two school-age children played with a ball a few feet away. The children ran to Scott, grasping his hands and giggling.

"Christine, this is Vera, Susan, and Roy." Scott grinned at the little group. His smile was contagious.

Vera had kind, sparkling eyes and a wide grin. "It's wonderful to meet you! I saw you stand up for Patty at her wedding. It was such a beautiful service and reception." Vera's voice matched her eyes with their sincerity. The children said hello and then begged to play catch in the open space not too far from the blanket.

Vera agreed with the warning, "Stay out of the road, please."

Christine and Scott joined Vera on the blanket. The three adults exchanged pleasantries and then shared the current events of their lives. Scott told Christine how until a year and a half before, he had simply existed, a shell of his former self who was unable to do more than take one day at a time. Although he came home from the war with no significant physical injuries, his mind had felt broken. He struggled with an extreme weight of guilt and anger at himself, which had led to long bouts of despair. He could not get himself out of bed many days and lost several jobs due to it.

This was the Scott Christine's mind pictured most of the past ten years. Several times through the years, she and Patty had eavesdropped on Mr. and Mrs. Meyer discussing Scott's woes in worried tones. The Meyers had been uncertain how to reach their son but longed to find a way to support and encourage him. Patty had desperately wanted the older brother back, who had teased her and brought home penny candy from the grocery store where he worked. Scott was seven years older than Patty, and before the war, had been full of fun and grand ideas. It had upset each of them to see Scott so altered and lost in a world they had no understanding of, or a way to help him wrestle free from the hold of depression.

Mockingbirds chirped and the grackles cawed in the trees surrounding them. A soft wind blew Christine's loose hair about, tickling her neck, and yet she was enraptured with Scott's story. He continued telling of how a veteran of the Great War invited him on a fishing trip with a few other men nearly two years ago. Scott did not know what inspired him to go with a group of strangers. It could have been that he was tired of sitting around his parents' house or that he sensed something had to change. Whatever the reason, Scott had gone with Bill Garrison and his crew. As they'd sat in a boat at 4:00 in the morning, Bill talked about his own experience assimilating into society when he came back to American soil once more.

Next thing Scott knew, he'd been crying and learning that the grace and redemption he had heard preached to him since childhood really did apply to him too. Over the following months, Bill and his friends had mentored Scott and helped him find a job at Ben E. Keith. For a while, Scott did not tell his parents or Patty that things had changed. He was different and really felt joy and satisfaction for the first time in his life. However, he was afraid that if he mentioned anything, the dream would end and the dark clouds of desperation and despair would return. Bill had assured Scott that his family would see the changes in time and that he could wait to tell them when he was ready.

Tears of joy brimmed in Christine's eyes. She knew what a victory it was for him experience such a breakthrough.

With beaming smiles, Scott and Vera mentioned how they met. Their mirth at the experience was palpable.

Vera had worked in the mail room at Ben E. Keith and Scott worked in accounts payable. For weeks on end, they ran into one another in the oddest ways. Their first meeting occurred when Scott had turned a corner quickly and bumped into Vera. All the packages and letters she carried went flying into the air and then came raining down upon them like confetti at a party. He had apologized profusely and helped pick up the fallen items. They both went on their way, glad to leave the incident behind until Vera's last stop was at his desk. They sheepishly exchanged names. Another time Vera had caught Scott trying and failing to unlock her car. It turned out they both drove the same 1946 white Chevrolet Clipper and his was parked seven spaces to the right. Scott had been embarrassed by his missteps around Vera and tried to avoid the mail room when he could.

Christine giggled at Scott's sheepish expression. She would have been mortified if she had been a similar position.

"I had asked a coworker to deliver any packets or paperwork that came through the mailroom for Scott," Vera admitted with a laugh. "It seemed the harder we worked to avoid one another the more circumstances brought us together."

Like two polarized magnets, they continued to be drawn to one another. They ran into each other at the lunch counter two days during one week. There was a staff picnic and they were assigned to the same team for games. Vera had fallen during the sack race and pulled Scott down as she tumbled to the ground. A few months later, Scott and Vera had discovered they went to the same church, though they usually attended different services, when Vera's son ran ahead and sat down in the pew beside Scott. Vera had blushed when she caught up and discovered that the back of the head that looked vaguely familiar did in fact belong to Scott.

"It was almost as if God was trying to make it very clear that we were meant to see one another." Scott chuckled. On that Sunday morning while they waited for the service to begin, Vera's son Roy asked Scott where his father was. Scott answered that his parents attended a church on the other side of town. Roy shared that his father had gone to heaven. Scott had squeezed the boy's shoulder, and his heart had grieved for the fatherless boy he did not know and for his mother who worked hard to raise her children. That Sunday began a tradition of sitting together in church. They added Sunday lunch together after a few weeks. Gradually, Scott and Vera discovered that their paths were now the same.

"We plan to make it official soon, but wanted to give Patty and Nelson their time in the spotlight," Vera said. "Every bride deserves her day to be celebrated." A sweet look passed between the couple.

It was uplifting to see Scott find happiness with someone as delightful as Vera. Christine was thrilled for him.

"Christine, I am so glad you stayed to visit with us," Scott said. "For so many years you saw me faltering and failing. I wanted to show you that if a guy like me can make it out of such despondency and start a wonderful new life, you can too. You have faced many tough challenges this year, the type that makes a person lose hope. I want you to see there is hope and joy to come. Sometimes there are bends and twists in our paths or you take a wrong way, but never forget redemption is always available to all."

Scott's advice stuck with Christine later that night as she lay in bed listening to Alice's soft feathery breath as she slept peacefully. Christine's path, the one she had dreamed of had washed away in the storms life had thrown her. Some days she feared what lay on the road ahead. How many obstacles and sharp twists were in her future? Not knowing what else to do since her course had shifted and she felt directionless, she would trudge on.

She paused at the thought. Lately, purpose bloomed. Helping with Pete's classes made her feel useful. Building friendships with the other volunteers and students gave her confidence. It was not the direction she anticipated a year ago, but it was beginning to feel like a better way.

Chapter 10

November 1955

At work, Dennis was engaged and energized by the challenge of his new role. He was respected and had even made a new friend who invited him to go fish in the Trinity River a time or two. Dennis discovered he should not rely on his fishing skills to supply his food, but he had a good time and enjoyed getting to know his coworker, Martin Krupsky, better. Martin and his wife, Camille, invited Dennis over for supper using the fish he and Martin had caught that morning before work.

It was one of the first dinners Dennis had been a part of where the whole family sat around the table and talked long after the meal ended. From the youngest to the oldest, each child was asked to share about their day at school and given the opportunity to tell some special fact or story about themselves with Dennis. Henry, the youngest boy proudly demonstrated how his tongue could wiggle his front tooth back and forth. The only daughter amongst the pack of boys was Annette. She was in fifth grade and explained her goal to become a nurse one day.

"I am always helping Mama patch up these rough boys so I have a lot of training already," she told Dennis very seriously.

Wyatt, their seventh grader was the quietest of the crew, but managed to share how much he liked collecting baseball cards. The oldest son, Rick, asked Dennis to attend his first high school basketball home game of the season that Friday night. At the end of the evening, Dennis thanked his gracious hosts. He left amazed at the idea that there were families who seemed to revel in one another's company. It made him think that having a family of his own someday might be something he could watch and learn how to do well at some point in the much distant future. Could be that if he did the opposite of his own rearing, things would turn out better, he thought wryly.

Dennis decided to join Martin and Camille's family to see Rick play on Friday night. He had only attended one basketball game during his entire time in high school but remembered liking the fast pace of the game. Martin told Dennis to meet them in the gymnasium of the new high school building for Paschal High School, which had moved its campus a few blocks west earlier that year. It was strange to hear the name of his alma mater associated with a different location, but Dennis supposed life was teaching him that things never stayed the same for long and change was inevitable. He was glad that the students had a brand new building.

When he arrived, the stands were filling quickly with fans. He searched the crowd until he spotted the fire-red swath of hair Martin was known around the office for having. Annette and Camille waved him over excitedly.

Dennis cheered extra loudly alongside the Krupsky family when Rick made a basket. The energy of the crowd in the stands was invigorating. Back and forth, the two teams battled for the lead. The Paschal Panthers took back the lead in the final minute of the game and held on to secure a victory. Rick and the whole team jumped around the court as the crowd of well-wishing fans surrounded them. Dennis was glad to have been part of such a good night.

As he shook hands with Martin and the other men around him as well as Rick, Dennis grasped that due to Myrna, Martin, and others, he was slowly becoming part of the community around him. It was an accomplishment he had rarely experienced in his twenty-six years.

Since the weather had cooled off, Myrna and Dennis resumed their Saturday morning coffee ritual while the mornings were crisp but not frigid. At least once a week, he joined Myrna, Leon, and Essie Mae—if she was not working—for a game of cards or checkers and dessert. He and Martin often ate lunch together in the bank's employee lounge if their schedules allowed it. Yet despite all of the new friendships, loneliness persistently crept into his hours alone at home, stealing Dennis's peace of mind.

In the hours on his own, guilt, shame, and despondency tore at the new life he was establishing. Guilt accused him of not grieving long or hard enough for Kay before seeking out happiness. Shame reminded Dennis he had failed Kay and that his faults had led to her tragic end. Despondency whispered that his life could not change, that he was doomed to an existence of broken relationships and failure.

Dennis did the best he could to focus on positive thinking but knew that he needed to get help from someone else. Even he knew that a person had to learn how to be comfortable on their own, at least some of the time. He had relied on Kay to make him happy and fill his life and calendar with excitement. She had done the same with him. When they could not measure up to each other's unquenchable expectations, they threw words like daggers at each other, wounding without care. Dennis was not sure if he was meant to be alone forever, but he was for now, and he was tired of the unsettling feeling that came over him when his mind was not occupied with work or friends. How could he understand his part in Kay's death and move forward without constantly facing guilt and shame? How could he learn to be at ease by himself?

One icy night, he and Myrna sat alone in her living room next to a crackling fire. Though he missed Essie Mae and Leon, Dennis was glad for the opportunity to ask Myrna the questions that had been on his mind for a while now. He had noticed photographs of Mr. Davis throughout her home. Their wedding picture hung proudly in the living room behind the loveseat. A picture of Mr. Davis in uniform sat on a small end table, and the kitchen boasted a more recent picture of the two of them, about fifteen years old based on the fashion.

"Myrna, you told me when we first met that you knew heartache. I'm thinking that heartache has a bit to do with your losing Mr. Davis. If you don't mind me asking, how do you get by and act so content and joyful though Mr. Davis is gone?" He would not have felt right asking anyone else such a personal question, but Dennis was secure in the fact that Myrna would not take offense.

126

Myrna smiled softly. "We have known each other a while now, son. I think it is about time to tell you my story." She paused before continuing. "I was born in 1873, just a few years since the war between the states ended. Times were tough then. It may be that they are always tough but our perspective changes as we experience more living." Myrna stopped again and stared at the picture of her husband. Dennis imagined she was thinking back over a half century of years gone by.

"Pap was a sharecropper on rented land near Ennis. Cotton mostly, but everybody planted a garden of beans and corn. There were eleven of us little ones living in a dirt sod house smaller than this one here. Was never much to live off of, despite how hard Ma and Pap worked. Ma insisted that all her children would have the chance to get an education if they wanted one. I think quitting school at a young age was one of her biggest regrets in life. My siblings and I walked miles to attend school. Our teacher, Ms. Conroe, found that I was gifted in Mathematics and Science. She and the school board raised money each year to sponsor one gifted child to go to high school in town. I won the scholarship and completed the program, then tested for my teaching certificate. I taught school children for nearly twenty years. The life of a female school teacher back then was a lonely one. My one room prairie school served town children, but most students came from nearby ranches and farms. I boarded with different families throughout the years. A few of them made a body feel like a part of the family, while others only wanted the housing stipend and any free labor they could get. Stepping out with a gentleman was forbidden for schoolmarms. I envied the girls whose papa could afford them and had the freedom to say yes to a caller, but I had no other respectable way to support myself or send money home for the family."

Dennis pictured a young Myrna and empathized for the poor girl who had put aside her dreams to support her family. It reminded him of how his older brother Miles had sacrificed so much to help his brothers and sister have life a little easier.

"In 1915, I had squirreled away enough cash to put myself through nursing school. I finished the schooling just in time to take care of our boys coming home from battling the Kaiser. Lloyd was one of my patients. He was wounded in the trenches of Germany and then caught the Spanish influenza on the boat ride home. Terrible sickness it was. None of the nurses and doctors were certain he would make it. Due to his injury, his body had fought hard for a long time. Surprisingly, Lloyd did make it and cheered everyone in the ward until he was released. I was as glad as everyone else, nothing more. I had quickly learned never to let myself get attached to patients. It was not proper or good for one's heart." Myrna stopped again to rest for a minute.

"A few months later, Lloyd happened to be working on a crew repairing the building next to the hospital. Sometimes, we would see each other on my way home to the boarding house from work. He would smile and wave or come say hello. Then one night he asked if I would like to have supper with him. I thought that I should turn him down—nurses' code and all—but I couldn't make my mouth say the words. During that supper, I learned he had married at twenty and within two years was the father of twin boys. Three years later, his wife and baby girl died during childbirth. Lloyd had raised his boys as best as he could with the help of his sister. Along the way, he joined the Army for a steady paycheck, which sent him to Europe to lead young men just a little older than his own boys. Two months after our first dinner together, Lloyd told me his next job was lined up back in Texas and would I please marry him so he didn't have to court me from afar."

A gentle smile played across Myrna's face. Dennis was pleased that his friend had experienced the pleasure of being pursued and loved.

"We were happy. I was in my mid-forties on our wedding day. We never had children of our own, but I enjoyed watching Lloyd's boys, Calvin and Robert, get married and have little ones. Though Lloyd's heart was weakened by the influenza, the Lord gave us twenty-two sweet years together before Lloyd passed. It was sudden. Lloyd went to help out at Calvin's place near Glen Rose. There was no way to get him to a hospital in time. I was angry by the time a neighbor came to get me hours later. There had been no goodbye. I ranted and screamed. I was hurt they took so long to bring me to Lloyd, though I would not have been able to save him. Things that should not be said were spewed in my anger. It was my first reaction, but not my truest feelings. The heat of the moment broke years of bonds between us all. Not long after, Calvin moved his family to California. It has taken years, but through letters we have found forgiveness."

Dennis could sense that telling her story had taken an emotional toll on Myrna. "Dennis, my boy," she said fondly. "There is forgiveness and peace to be had if you want it. But you have to believe it, let Christ change you. Then you get to experience real joy. It's unlike fleeting happiness. Joy carries you, though the path has bumps—deep ruts even. I hope you'll think about what I said."

He promised to think on her story and kept coming back to her words in the hours when there was no one but himself for company. Was he willing to believe in the hope Myrna told him about? Could he, a man who had made so many mistakes, really experience true joy again as Myrna did?

Sitting down and reading through the newspaper from beginning to end was one pastime Dennis picked up while in the Army. When his unit had down time, Dennis read the entirety of any U.S. newspaper he could get his hands on. With no one but his sister, Janet, to write to, he did not get much information about life in the United States except from hearsay and gossip from other soldiers. Sometimes he craved stories about people and places that were familiar and peaceful, while other times he preferred an article that made him think or taught him something new or a different perspective. Often times, he found the stories in old copies of newspapers he found at the USO tent or that were passed from another soldier. At the time, he had felt so desperate for news from his homeland. It fed a need in his soul, like oxygen for a drowning man. Looking back, it had been connection that he had been lacking—connection to someone who knew who he was as a person and cared to know more than his name, rank, and unit number. He had not taken the time to read the paper much since returning stateside. Meeting Kay had filled the yawning void in his life, for a time.

On Monday evening, the week before Thanksgiving, Dennis was reading the current events section of the newspaper when there was a banging on his front door. He heard a muffled, breathless voice calling his name. He peered through the peephole to see Myrna's figure raising her hand to beat on the door again.

He opened the door, "Myrna, what's wrong? Are you all right?"

"Oh, Dennis, help me! Come quickly, it's Leon. He's in the kitchen," she said in a hurried manner.

Dennis quickly pulled the door shut and ran across the lawn to Myrna's; her front door was ajar so he slipped in and found a very still Leon lying on the floor. A small pool of blood had seeped onto the floor from the gash in the swollen bump on the back of Leon's skull and cut on his forehead. Dennis felt dizzy. His stomach revolted, violently threatening to send its contents outward. Before Kay's death, he hadn't been squeamish about blood. He had to focus—for Leon's sake. Leon's soft rasping breaths brought him to the present. The shallow gulps gave him relief while he began his gentle examination. He removed the cloth rag from Leon's mouth, guessing he would be safe without it now that the seizing had stopped. Myrna handed Dennis a clean cloth to stop the blood flow. There were no other apparent injuries, but Dennis did not like the fact that Leon showed no signs of regaining consciousness.

"Have you called Frank's to reach Essie Mae yet?" he asked.

"No, I came to get you as soon as the shaking stopped, and I had cleaned him a bit. Head wounds bleed a lot, so no surprise it's started again. Figured you had some training in the Army due to assisting the medics and could help me. It's been a long time since I doctored anybody." Dennis kept his attention on Leon. "I have looked at what I know to, but have no experience with these sorts of things. I'm thinking we should call Essie Mae and see if she thinks we should take him to the hospital."

She nodded. "Mrs. Neilson, two doors down has a telephone line. I'll ask her to use it if you watch over our boy."

He agreed.

The minutes waiting for Myrna's return ticked by slowly. Leon had yet to move with the exception of the gentle rise and fall of his chest. He managed to stop the blood flow and carefully set about cleaning the wound and the floor underneath without moving Leon but a fraction. He remembered the Army medics telling him not to move a soldier too much before they had time to assess the injury. Only in the heat of battle when there was no time, all options but getting them out of the line of fire were off the table.

Myrna came back slightly winded from the trek in the dark. "Essie Mae says he isn't usually unconscious this long and thinks we should head to the hospital. Can you drive and pick up Essie Mae on the way? She is going to start walking and hope to meet us in the middle."

As tenderly as possible, Dennis carried Leon's prone form out to the car. Myrna sat in the backseat and held Leon's head and upper body on her lap. Dennis drove as smoothly as he could manage while maintaining a good speed. They spotted Essie Mae three blocks away and pulled over for her to get in the front seat.

On the way to the hospital, Myrna explained what happened, "He was sitting in a kitchen chair eating a cookie when he started shaking all of a sudden. I figured he was having one of his seizures, so I ran over from washing dishes at the sink, but I couldn't make it in time before he hit the front of his head on the table's edge and then slammed the back on the chair as he fell to the floor. I laid him on his side like you said to and put a dish cloth in his mouth to keep him from biting his tongue. I tried smelling salts after the shaking stopped, but it didn't faze him one bit. I couldn't think what else to do, so I ran and got

Dennis once Leon appeared to be fine enough to leave for the moment." Myrna's voice sounded laden with regret.

"These days, my nurses' training don't stick in my head the way it used to. It's been nearly thirty years since I practiced last. I'm sorry, Essie Mae."

Kindly, Essie Mae assured her friend, "Myrna, don't blame yourself. You did exactly what you could and should have. With Leon not coming to yet, the doctors will have to run their tests."

Hospital workers rushed out to meet their car at the curb because Essie Mae had called ahead before leaving Frank's. Leon was wheeled off to be examined with Essie Mae following closely behind.

Dennis helped Myrna from the backseat. She looked worn-out, so he asked if he could drive her back home. She opted to stay, saying she wanted to be with Essie Mae when she heard an update.

Dennis was unsure whether he could handle stepping foot into the hospital again. The ambulance drivers had brought Kay to this same place: John Peter Smith Hospital.

A queasy feeling welled up inside him. His thoughts wrestled one another. He wanted to support his friends, but the memories of this place overwhelmed him.

His mind flashed back to the night of the accident. He was sitting on the damp pavement of the curb, his pant seat soaked through. The ambulance driver asked him if he would like to ride in the back with Kay or follow behind them. He chose to drive his car. Though he had sat with other bodies waiting for final transport over in Korea, he could not bear the thought of being trapped in the ambulance with his damaged, lifeless Kay. It made the accident seem too real. So, with shaking hands, he had started the car's ignition and pulled out onto the street to follow behind the somber procession. The ambulance

THE PATHS WE WALK

drivers did not switch on their lights like they usually did when transporting someone to the hospital. They did not have to. There was no emergency. Kay was gone. Even his numb mind had registered the hospital as a formality while pulling into to a parking space. The strong antiseptic smell burned his nose upon entry. At the front desk, he'd told the registration matron that he was with the ambulance. She had looked at him stoically and directed him to the morgue. Taking one step after another had been all his mind could will his body to do.

Sirens blaring in his ear pulled Dennis back to the present. He was here now and could not stay outside all night in the cold air. Besides, he did not want to worry Myrna and Essie Mae anymore than they were already. Slowly, he took the path to the hospital, step by weighted step. The familiar stringent odor greeted him at the door. He pushed down the queasiness and trudged over to where the women waited. Essie Mae looked relieved to see him but also compassionate toward his plight. She thanked him again for bringing them and updated him on the little they knew. It was not much. The nurses had examined Leon and promised that the doctor would do so shortly and order a few tests to be run too.

Essie Mae told Dennis that Leon had fallen from the step ladder while dusting a shelf at work this morning. "He has dusted at least once a week for the past three years. I'm not sure what caused him to misstep or lose his balance, but he fell hard on his shoulder. Mr. Anderson called me at the office to make sure I knew, but Leon insisted on staying. I thought he was embarrassed but fine, so I went ahead and walked him to Myrna's and went on to my shift at Frank's. The fall must have jarred him more than I thought." She winced, clearly regretting much of the evening.

Dennis paced the small waiting area as the minutes turned to hours. He could read the apprehension on Essie Mae's face and see the disheartened stoop to Myrna's shoulders. Finally, they received the all clear from the doctors just after midnight. Leon would need to stay overnight for observation since he had been unconscious and hard to revive for almost an hour. All of the other tests showed results that were typical for Leon.

"Go home and rest, Ms. Kuntz, and call us in the morning for an update before heading over," Dr. Andrews said.

Leon made a quick recovery and was released the following afternoon with the instructions to rest and avoid lifting and strenuous work. Given his language barriers, Leon could not tell any of them what happened but he was able to communicate that he wanted to go to work. Dr. Andrews thought that he could sweep and pick light objects around the store by the following week. "But let his boss know not to let him overdo things or get on a step ladder for a while," Dr. Andrews warned Essie Mae, who privately told Dennis and Myrna that she would leave the decision of when Leon went back to work up to their parents.

Thanksgiving Day of 1955 was downright frigid. The roads were slick with ice, yet Dennis felt snug and content with his friends near. Under Myrna's careful tutelage, Dennis learned how to bake a turkey complete with stuffing. Growing up, his family had been too poor to afford many holiday trimmings. He and Kay had not bothered with what some folks called traditional Thanksgiving dinner. Only in the Army had he eaten all the "fixings" on the holiday.

Myrna said they would do things up especially big to cheer Essie Mae and Leon, who decided to forego the long trip to the farm this year due to Leon's unexplainable seizure the prior week. His parents and Essie Mae worried the long, bumpy car ride might initiate more trauma and add to the mound of medical bills they already faced.

Essie Mae waited tables at Frank's three nights each week in addition to working forty hours a week at her bookkeeping job. Dennis worried for her working herself so hard, but he did not have a better solution. He had passed her name and information on to the bank's hiring manager a few weeks before hoping that something would come of it before long.

Despite the foul weather and hardships, the four of them had eaten well, played games, and popped corn to share while listening to a special holiday-themed radio broadcast. After reveling in the communion of being with those you hold dear, Leon drifted off to sleep soon after dinner. Essie Mae told them he had been sleeping poorly this week and she did not want to disturb him even to walk the block home to his bed. They all talked quietly in the kitchen, until Myrna showed signs of being weary too. Dennis and Essie Mae assured Myrna they were capable of washing dishes and cleaning up the kitchen and encouraged her to lie down and rest. Myrna and Dennis had started the turkey at 5:00 o'clock that morning. Dennis knew Myrna had to be exhausted because even he kept yawning when he hoped none of them would notice.

While they washed and dried the pots and pans, Dennis was enjoying the time talking with Essie Mae one on one too much to share how tired he was. They moved around the tiny kitchen harmoniously, setting everything to right. Dennis was disturbed when the thought that Essie Mae would look good in his almost identical kitchen floated into his brain. Quite possibly, it was more disturbing that he found the thought so pleasant and difficult to let go. It took root through the rest of the afternoon, causing him to stumble over his answers and making his face heat when she looked at him. Dennis was trying to come up with a good excuse to leave when Myrna suggested they use Dennis's car to transport a now groggy Leon home.

The panicked, awkward feelings subsided when Dennis returned to his own home. He chastised himself for thinking of Essie Mae in that manner considering that Kay had been gone less than a year. Besides, he told himself, Essie Mae probably would not want him anyway. She had enough on her plate without adding a widower with a staggering load of guilt.

Still, his brain persisted in thinking about her. Essie Mae was just about the kindest, most genuine woman he had ever met. She was not plain like he had originally thought. Her golden brown hair and pale gray green eyes gave her a subtle, pure beauty. She would never be described as flashy, but was pretty nonetheless. Even if she did have feelings for him, it was too soon, he sternly reminded himself. There was Leon to think of too. Would he want another man in his sister's life? The questions swirled in Dennis's mind until, at last, he slept peacefully.

Chapter 11

November 1955

The days of November passed quickly for Christine. Dr. Bedford and Dr. Evans added another partner to their dental practice. Dr. Evans's nephew, Alan, joined the practice, adding new patients and a higher volume of paperwork to be typed and filed. Louise, who had been their part-time dental assistant agreed to work full time. Still, Louise and Margaret hoped the doctors would hire another part-time hygienist soon. All of their hours were long due to the changes.

Though she loathed to do so, Christine missed two Tuesday night classes, due to staying late at the office to type up new patient's files. Pete understood and assured Christine he would help her students and that her presence would be missed.

The younger Doctor Evans reminded Christine of Bryan in several aspects. He was tall, athletic, smart, and confident, and he gave her the impression that he understood how to use his charm to get what he wanted. Soon after he joined the practice, there was an influx of new female patients between the ages of eighteen and twenty five years.

One particularly trying afternoon, Margaret grumbled, "I wish someone would drag him to the altar already and be done with it. I'm tired of all these simpering southern belles coming in here like we are running a salon or match-making service."

Christine agreed. She left with an aching head many days after trying to juggle her additional workload and all the extra demands the new patients had. She knew that it was only a matter of time until they fell back into a rhythm and the new files were in proper order, so she put on a smile and got to work.

After a few weeks, the harried busyness did slow, although Christine began to feel ill at ease for another reason. Though she had spent time trying to piece it all together, Christine could not yet put a finger on what about the young Dr. Evans set her on edge. Perhaps she was jaded from her experience with Bryan. In her head, she knew that simply because a man was wealthy, well sought after, or sophisticated, it did not equate to his being untrustworthy or having a major flaw in his character. Christine had personally experienced how hurtful and harmful others' unfounded judgment could be. She promised herself to be kind and fair to the young man who was far from home and just beginning his career.

As the days passed, Alan, as he had asked to be called when not in front of patients, continued to use his charm on the mothers and daughters of Fort Worth. Christine knew from overhearing patients' chatter that he would take one girl to hear the orchestra, another to the movies, and still one more out to dinner and dancing. His actions ignited her feelings of distrust once more, but there was not much else Christine could do about it except to be on her guard. For now, Christine did her best to ignore the clients' gossip and try not to spread hearsay to Margaret and Louise when they talked on their lunch break.

On the Friday, a week before Thanksgiving, Christine decided to take in a motion picture by herself. She wanted to see the film *To Catch a Thief* weeks earlier, but had missed seeing it with Alice and their older sister Elizabeth, due to another late night at work. Both sisters had raved about the film afterward.

That afternoon, Christine told Margaret that she had decided to be brave and not rely on others for enjoyment. She figured a woman of twenty-two years old should feel secure enough to be seen on her own at a movie theater. Mom had a light supper prepared by the time Christine and her Dad arrived home from their offices. They all ate a quick bite before heading out to their own evening plans. Alice was off to a Heights' basketball game with her friends and her parents walked down the block to play board games with Mr. and Mrs. Meyer and another couple from the neighborhood.

Christine had always enjoyed motion pictures. She appreciated the care and hard work that went into making such masterpieces. Growing up, she and Patty liked to imagine themselves as costume and set designers. They put together extravagant outfits and set designs and often roped Alice and Fred—the Hinkle's dog at the time—into starring roles. Those had been such good, uncomplicated days!

Christine was just locking her car in the theater parking lot when she heard a familiar, masculine voice calling her name. It was Pete Ashby. She had only seen him briefly in passing these last few weeks.

"Hi, stranger!" his usual grin in place let her know he did not begrudge her busyness of late.

Christine laughed along with him. "I was trying to avoid you and use work as an excuse," she joked. His smile back reassured her that he understood that she teased him right back.

They walked into the theater's spacious lobby. The buttery smell of popcorn wafted through the air. From the heavy velvet draperies to the sleek geometric designs running along the walls and ceiling to the wall sconces casting a milky glow, the place was charming and cozy. Christine loved the comfortable feeling the old theater evoked in her.

"What movie are you seeing tonight?" Pete asked as they neared the ticket counter.

"*To Catch a Thief.* I was supposed to see it with my sisters but duty called. They raved about it for weeks. Patty and Nelson, Margaret and Louise, even Carol Ann and my mom have all seen it too. So I decided to come see it by myself."

"Would you mind if I join you?" Pete questioned. "I haven't seen it yet either, and I'm always game for a Cary Grant film."

"That would be nice! I put on a brave face telling everyone I would go to a movie on my own, but the truth is that they are really so much better when you can share them with someone," Christine replied.

Pete agreed and told her that his roommate's parents were in town for a visit and that he had left the small apartment to give them time alone, but had not planned much farther than coming to the theater. They smiled at each other and went to get tickets.

He insisted on paying. "You have done so much for our students and program. It's the least I can do," he said, although Christine assured Pete he did not need to and that helping the students was bringing more happiness to her life than in a long while.

Pete asked if he could get her anything to snack on during the movie. Christine told him she was fine, but if he offered her a piece or two of what he was having, she would happily oblige him. He headed over to join the line for the concession counter while Christine examined the large movie posters hanging on the walls to entice fans to see more films.

One poster for the recently released but relatively controversial film *Rebel Without a Cause* drew Christine's attention. She stared at the striking, handsome face of the hard-edged, young motion picture star, James Dean, who had died just shy of two months earlier in a tragic, automobile accident. His soulful eyes and poignant expression made Christine feel sorry for the man who had left the world so prematurely. An insistent tug luring Christine to be pulled back into the swirling eddies of guilt and shaming thoughts and emotions from her own accident threatened to grip her mind.

Christine shook her head to clear the futile thoughts and moved on to the next poster. It advertised a film promising intrigue and suspense. The western-themed poster beside it promoted a new Charleston Heston and Jane Wyman film. Then, for the second time that evening, Christine heard a male voice say her name.

"Christine, what a pleasure to run into you here," Alan said so near to her ear that Christine jumped a bit at the sound of his voice. "Are you seeing *To Catch a Thief*? The ushers have begun seating people now. Let's go grab seats before all the good spots are taken." He grabbed Christine's elbow and began to tug her toward the theater.

Christine's discomfort grew at his overly familiar behavior. How could she get out of this uncomfortable situation? Her eyes searched for and landed on Pete who was walking back with a bag of peanuts and a box of Cracker Jacks. Pete sized up the circumstance and seemed to understand Christine's distress.

"Hi, I'm Pete Ashby. I've not met you." Pete stuffed the snacks in his coat pocket and held out his hand. Proper etiquette forced Alan to remove his hand from Christine's arm to shake Pete's. Smooth as a knife cutting butter, Pete shook Alan's hand and slid his left arm around Christine's shoulder, drawing her to his side.

"We had better get in; looks like it's about time for the film to start. It was nice meeting you, Alan." With that, Pete's warm hand guided Christine into the theater.

Several times throughout the film, Christine's eyes searched the audience around the theater for Alan. If he was there, she could not locate him in the dim lighting. She had not meant to be hurtful, but he should not have been so assuming. However, there was nothing she could do about it tonight, so she figured she might as well not let worry take away the pleasure of the film.

Pete shared the Cracker Jacks and peanuts as promised. He even gave her the prize at the bottom too. She laughed when he handed her the little resin charm of a circus clown. Christine was thankful for the darkness of the theater because she blushed more than a few times when their fingers brushed while reaching for a piece or handing the snack containers to one another.

As the lights in the theater rose from dim to bright, Christine agreed that all of her friends and family were right. Cary Grant and Grace Kelly were fantastic in their roles. Their chemistry, the plot, and the acting was superb. Christine would count it among her favorite motion pictures, which was saying a lot, because she adored movies.

Seeing the film with Pete made the night even better. She could not imagine having such a comfortable or enjoyable experience with Dr. Alan. Being the gentleman he was, Pete walked her to her car, where they continued to discuss their favorite parts of the movie, which led to more talk about much-loved films and books.

They discovered they preferred many of the same stories and authors. The night air was chilly but the warmth of their camaraderie made Christine want to stay out forever. That is, until they looked around and noticed that somehow the lot around them had emptied and their cars were the last two left. Christine's watch read 12:32 a.m.

"Oh, my mom will be worried. I must get home. Pete, thank you for tonight… for everything… for inviting me to be part of your classes. It means a lot to me." She smiled and gave him a small hug. Then she wished him goodnight and started her car.

On the car ride home, Christine admitted to herself for the first time that Pete had come to mean very much to her. She deeply admired his faith and his conviction to serve others in their community. She also found him quite attractive. His charismatic smile cheered her and gave her a sense that each moment was full of bright opportunities. Though these were new revelations, the thoughts were comforting, like sitting curled up in a warm blanket with a good book on a winter day. It felt natural and peaceful, luxurious and sweet.

In high school, Christine had not known Pete very well, although they had a few classes together throughout the years. She imagined that most of their peers and teachers would have described him as outgoing, but Christine had thought him a bit shy when they worked on projects together. Other than that, she knew Pete had been respected and won whatever leadership role he campaigned for. He was always right up there academically with Sheila, all while working an after school job shelving groceries at Roy Pope's.

Sheila. Christine's heady discovery of feelings came crashing back to reality. Pete never mentioned Shelia much. Sheila rarely referenced him in her letters, except to ask about how her classes were going. What were Pete and Sheila to each other? Christine ached to know. Her time with Pete the past three months and tonight had been unlike any during the year and a half she and Bryan saw each other. Pete was considerate and funny. When he smiled, he made a body feel like they should too. He worked hard and gave of himself generously. He might not wear an expensive suit or have the "right connections," but his gray blue eyes and rich brown hair were the kind of handsome that drew her in.

She had spent countless hours in Bryan's company but was never allowed to see the man behind the façade. She knew only the outward image he presented and what she could interpose from watching him interact with his family, friends, and society at large. Christine thought she could have kept on seeing him, maybe even married Bryan and had a family without ever truly understanding what motivated his actions and satisfied his soul. How could she have been so blinded by his outward appearance and wealth that she missed the realization that she did not know the real Bryan?

She pulled into the driveway, but lingered at her car for a moment still thinking about Pete. He was constantly drawing people in, and willing to honestly share about himself. He was humble too. One of the students asked why he chose to be an electrician if he was so smart. He had replied, "When I was young, my part of the city often had power outages and the people lived in unsafe conditions. Although we were able to move to another area, many families from the neighborhood were not. As an electrician for the city, I am able to be a part of making Fort Worth a better place to live and helping kids from homes like my first one have lights to see by after dark." His answer had challenged Christine to see the ways she could do more for those who lived around her. Helping at the classes was a start, but truthfully she wanted to reach more people than those who attended.

Christine quietly opened the back door of her parents' house, hoping that Harry would not bark and wake her family. As she crept to the living room to turn off the glow of the lamp, she noticed her mother, who had fallen asleep in a living room chair. Christine regretted that she had made her mom wait and worry again. It did not seem fair that at nearly twenty-three her mom still had to fear what could happen to her on a regular Friday night in the sleepy town of Fort Worth.

Christine's mind trailed off, wondering how Kay Oswald's mother was doing these days. Was she wracked with fear anytime her remaining child or grandchildren were out and about? With morbid curiosity, Christine had found a newspaper and read a copy of Kay's obituary. It read that Kay was survived by her husband, mother, and a brother and sister-in-law who had several children. Christine had thought about them through the months. She ached to share how sorry she was with them. She and her parents debated the merits of her sending a letter to the family. In the end, they had encouraged Christine to write the letter and to mail it when she felt peace that it was the right time and the message she wished to share. The letter had been written and revised dozens of times now, but Christine found it lacking. It would never be enough. A piece of paper would not replace the loss of their dear one's life. The words "I am so sorry" could never be sufficient. When she allowed herself to dwell on that fact, Christine was weighed down with guilt, and so the copies of the letter lay buried under sweaters in her bottom dresser drawer.

She snapped herself out of her thoughts and gently rubbed her mother's arm and urged her to go to bed. As her mom's hazy, sleep-heavy eyes began to focus again, Christine felt guilty once more at the great relief on her mother's unguarded face. Like a heavy burden had been lifted from her, if even for a moment's time.

Christine tiptoed through her nightly bed time routine, trying not to wake her sister. Alice must have been sleeping lightly or sensed her movements, because Christine looked over to see her sister's large hazel eyes watching her.

"You are home late." It was a statement with a question underneath.

"Yes, I ran into a friend at the theater. We decided to see the movie together and got to talking afterward." Had it been more lit in the room, Christine's crimson blush would have given away that it had been no ordinary friend or evening.

Alice was no fool. She was observant by nature and a lover of anything that hinted at romance. "Would this friend happen to be a man?" she questioned slyly.

The girlish side of Christine bubbled inside her. How she longed to share with her sister that it had been the man of her dreams, and the evening had been engaging and wholesome, a meeting of two souls who seemed to complement and enhance each other. With Christine uncertain of Sheila's role in the big picture, she held her tongue about the matter.

"It was just a friend, but I enjoyed catching up and discussing *To Catch a Thief*. Y'all were right—the acting was divine. I have always adored Cary Grant's charming accent. It's enough to make a girl swoon."

Alice leaned closer to where Christine sat on the matching twin bed to her own. She examined her older sister for a minute. A look of hurt crossed her beautiful face. "I'm not a little girl anymore. You and Elizabeth have always treated me like a baby because I am so much younger. Mom and Dad, all of you, can't seem to get past the fact that I have grown up. You come in here practically floating on air and I can tell. I have seen you on some of your worst days and tonight is not one of them. You don't want to tell me about the guy you like? Fine. You are entitled to some privacy. But, please know, I am not some child who needs to be shielded from the difficulties of life. I have listened to you cry yourself to sleep night after night, yet you hold it all in. You hardly rely on anyone. I am here, ready to listen, and I care. I want to help. Please stop shutting me out." With that, Alice flopped on her other side, facing the wall.

Despite the late hour, sleep would not come to Christine. Her sister was right for the most part. She and her parents spoke about the accident in hushed tones, rarely bringing up the topic around Alice. When Elizabeth and her husband visited from Hurst or James and Carol Ann came over, they all waited to discuss the issue when Alice was out of the room or gone to see friends. Phillip was away at Texas Agriculture and Mechanical University, but the scenario was the same during his visits. Each of them tried to shelter Alice from the pain of life. Sadly, they did her no favor. Soon enough, every person had to learn some lessons through pain and challenge. It was the way the world worked; there was no getting around it.

Christine was saddened to learn how acutely aware of their unmindful actions her sweet, younger sister was. She vowed to remedy it tomorrow by taking the time needed to share her thoughts and emotions about the accident and the events following. In truth, Alice had been living through them alongside Christine already. It was time to expose the sordid details, and let her sister understand the hardships as well as the healing process. The topic of Pete would remain off limit for the present. It was too new and uncertain. Christine did not understand completely how to feel about it and that was more than she wanted to delve into with her high school age sister, even if she was wiser than they all gave her credit for.

For the time being, Christine lay in bed, her thoughts drifting toward Alice, Pete, Sheila, and Alan. Christine's mind worked out scenarios of Pete and Sheila together, then Pete not having any interest in Sheila while Sheila pined for him and vice versa, and finally, the two of them being only friends, making way for her and Pete to live happily ever after. Christine wished the final thought was the truest one.

Her restless mind then probed Alan Evans's appearance at the theater and his uncomfortable assumption that they would see the film together, which also mystified her. He had never asked to speak with her outside work or sought out her company after hours. It could be their meeting was a coincidence and he just wanted a friend to see the film with. His presumption still bothered her, if this was the most accurate theory.

When sleep finally came, her dreams were a confusing jumble of all of her reasoning. The figures of each person would show up in the oddest places and say things that would hopefully never come to fruition. It was not a restful night to say the least.

Christine woke to find Alice still asleep. She knew her sister had tossed and turned the night through, because she had been awake much of the time she was not dreaming. The need to reconcile with Alice pressed on Christine until she tapped her sister's shoulder lightly.

"Alice? Would you be up for spending the day with me? I thought we could drive to Dallas to have lunch and shop until our arms are loaded with bags and packages."

Alice came fully awake at the pronouncement that shopping would be involved. "You know I am not a kid that you can bribe with a little bit of food and a fun activity." Her sober tone revealed the hurt from last night would take care and time to restore.

"That's fair," Christine replied. "How about we talk the whole drive there and back? There are things about the accident and afterwards that I want to tell you and explain in my own way."

Alice studied her face. "Are you serious or just trying to appease me?" *Wow! Her sister had grown up.* Christine was proud of the intelligent and spunky young woman before her.

"This is the real deal, kid!" She teased Alice, much like she was known to do in days gone by.

Alice grinned. "The day a girl turns down shopping and time with her older sister is a sad day. Let's go!"

On Monday at lunch, Christine went down to the five and dime around the corner to fill the list of ingredients Mom needed for Thanksgiving dinner. Mom worried that if they waited too long, the stores would be out of stock and her stuffing would be no good. As she walked up to the front door, Christine smiled at and greeted the young man sweeping the sidewalk. This was not her regular neighborhood store, but each time she visited, Christine enjoyed seeing this particular worker whose smile and joy was evident for all. After experiencing so many frowns and tight-lipped looks this year, a smile was no longer a simple blessing she took for granted.

Due to her lunchtime errand, there had not been time to take a walk around the block with Margaret as they did when they wanted privacy to talk, or gossip, if Christine was honest. She wanted to tell Margaret about Friday night, and from the looks Margaret had been sending her, Christine knew she was suspicious something was up.

"Take a walk around the block with me first?" Margaret asked as they left at the end of the day. Once they had walked out of hearing distance from the office, Margaret stopped her. "What was going on today? I noticed that Dr. Alan did not loiter at your desk sipping yet another cup of coffee nor did he come to 'check in about a patient' the usual ten times a day." Margaret said it with a teasing lilt to her voice, but an undercurrent of probing ran through the statement too.

Christine told Margaret about Alan's forward and presumptuous behavior on Friday night. "It makes no sense. The man has debutants and their mothers falling at his feet all day. I know he goes out with them because I hear chatter from the waiting room all day."

Margaret frowned. "On Friday afternoon, he came in just as Louise and I were discussing the film. She enjoyed it so much, and I told her you were going to see it that night. I hope our conversation did not lead to your trouble."

"It's unlikely." Christine reassured her. "I could be making a big deal out of nothing. If it is the case, I don't know how to feel about him assuming I was going alone. I'm glad Pete was there." Christine put her head down when the heat began seeping into her face.

Margaret grinned slyly. "I certainly am glad too. It's good to see you finding joy in life again. Even before the accident, Bryan squelched you, always critiquing you and telling you who to be. Your Pete starting that program to help the community makes him a great guy in my book."

"He's not my Pete. Honestly, I don't understand what Sheila and Pete are to each other, so I don't know if he will ever be. At Patty's wedding, I assumed they were together. Occasionally, she mentions him in her letters. You should have heard how proudly she talked about him at the wedding. It might mean something or might not, but how does a girl go about asking someone who lives a thousand miles away? I won't begin to pretend I am a literary savant who has perfected the art of prying information out subtly via letter. I am certainly not going to ask Pete. Sheila is taking the train home for Christmas. So even if it kills me, I'm stuck waiting. You had better believe I am going to do my best to get it out of her then."

"It's nice to see you scheming again too. For a while, I thought we lost that part of you." Margaret grinned and hugged Christine.

Christine laughed, "I have missed that part of me too." Then she sobered. "I do still think about Kay Oswald and her husband a lot. He looked so devastated waiting helplessly on the sidewalk. For so many months, the guilt has eaten at me. For a long while, I dreamed and would see Kay's face poking out in different scenes and situations. It would have been comical if it was someone else. I did not feel like I had the right to enjoy life or be comfortable and happy when I had caused such pain for others. I think volunteering with the classes has been good for me. I have stopped seeing myself as the victim of a circumstance. I have learned that many people, including those in my own city, live hard lives and face difficult decisions and situations every day. At times, they live without food or beds in cramped one-room apartments, unsure of how to provide more for those they love. Many have little control over their lives, yet they are living, striving for a better life. It has made me grateful for what I have and helped me focus on what I can change." It was a long speech, but Christine wanted to share how she was learning and growing and changing little by little.

"I am glad, honey! To look beyond your own pain and problems and give of yourself is a powerful gift to all involved." Margaret's affirmation brought a bit more healing to Christine's soul. When their block loop was complete, they said goodbye near their cars and left.

Thanksgiving Day at the Hinkle house was always a grand affair, and this year was no exception. The turkey was basted and stuffed, then placed in the oven to roast. Since the night before, Mom had Alice and Christine crafting pies and casseroles to run down to the Meyers' house for baking the next morning.

Typically, the Meyer family went to Patty's grandparent's home and was gracious enough to lend the use of their oven each year. With her grandmother in poor health, the torch was passed to a new generation. Mrs. Meyer had asked Patty if she would do the honor of playing hostess this year and then they would rotate after that, especially with Vera joining the family soon. Patty was thrilled to host this year. She had begun planning weeks earlier and had called Christine five times to go over ideas and discuss her final menu. Christine was proud of Patty for taking on such a big role, and knew her friend was up for the challenge.

This holiday was more special for the two Hinkle sisters living at home. Since their talk and day together, Alice and Christine were closer than ever before. They laughed and chatted as they baked food at the Meyers'. It was so good to be able to share life's serious details as well as silly things her students said during Sunday school, her thoughts on fashion or movies, and so much more. Christine would miss Alice when she headed to university to begin her teacher training next fall. She promised herself that she would write to her sister and work to keep them close, even when they were miles apart.

Philip had driven in from College Station the night before. Christine marveled at how mature looking he had become. He had worked for an oil company out near Odessa this past summer and had only been home for two short visits before returning to college in the fall. It was good to have him home. He played board games and stayed up late talking with Christine and Alice. The evening had been like so many in high school when just the youngest three Hinkle children were living at home. Christine reveled in the comfort and sweetness of their time together.

Around one o'clock Thanksgiving Day, James, Carol Ann, and baby Michael were the first to arrive. Carol Ann was beginning to show signs of her pregnancy, a gentle mound revealed that a little life growing inside. However, that had not stopped her from cooking quite a bit. They came bearing brisket and Carol Ann's delicious carrot cake; both dishes were a favorite with the Hinkle family. James often teased that he had married Carol Ann for her skills in the kitchen. She would roll her eyes and tell him he would be hopeless and hungry without her.

Elizabeth and her husband, Anthony, came next, bringing Aunt Ellen with them. These additions rounded out the group this year, because Michelle had wanted to host the Dallas side of the family, and Stephen was now engaged to a gal whose family had invited his family to their ranch up near Denton.

Even without their extended family, space was limited in the house. However, after raising five children in the home, Mom and Dad knew how to make good use of every inch. Due to the freezing temperatures, tables and chairs had been set up in the living room. Dad said a prayer and the food line began. Each dish was delicious. Christine was particularly proud of her iced cake. She had not left out the eggs or burned it like she had been known to do in past years.

By three o'clock, all bellies were satisfied. The men helped with dishes and then bundled up and headed outside to stretch their legs and play a game of horseshoes in the backyard.

The women rested in the living room, with Michael for entertainment. He had woken up from his nap and was eager to explore the house to see what he could get into. His tumble from the table was a distant memory for him and he was ready for trouble again. The ladies corralled him in the living room, but the happy little guy did not seem to mind as long as all eyes were on him. His chubby legs propelled him from person to person. When he arrived at the next participant, Michael would stick out his little belly and wait to be tickled before squealing and running away. This game went on until he became bored of it.

Christine's ears perked up when Mom and Carol Ann began discussing motherhood. If ever there was a good mother, it was hers. In the past year of raising Michael, Carol Ann had shown that she too had the instinct and making of a great mother.

Mom was saying, "Everyday there is this tension between not wanting to hold a child so close that they feel suffocated or fail to learn lessons on their own and taking the time to savor each sweet moment with them because you know life will never be quite the same again."

The statement stayed with Christine the rest of the day. She was so grateful both on this Thanksgiving Day and each day for her parents and family, her friends, home, and job. This year had been difficult and full of despair, but those who loved her had stood by and held her close while encouraging her to embrace and savor life yet again. She had much to be thankful for and determined to delight in all the sweet moments to come, whatever they may be.

Chapter 12

December 1955

This was the busiest December Dennis ever remembered experiencing. Work was hectic with preparing for and leading employee reviews—a first for Dennis to experience from the management side. He made careful notes on each of the four employees that reported to him, and together he and Mr. Mackenzie talked with the workers and shared what their annual bonus would be. Not all the reviews had been easy to give, but Dennis believed they were fair and honest. When the final review was finished, he was relieved and grateful to Mr. Mackenzie for mentoring him through the process.

In addition to the added responsibility at work, Myrna had recruited Dennis to help with the Christmas food pantry baskets at her church.

Dennis recollected years ago when a kind, well-meaning neighbor brought a similar basket to his home.

His mother took the basket timidly and hid the contents, subtly doling the items out piece by precious piece so his father would not take notice. Pop was adamant about refusing what he considered charity. Dennis was glad he could be a part of a program that brought joy to others, even if it was only for a small fraction of their day. He remembered how he, Miles, Janet, and Terry savored the caramel candies and peppermint sticks that had been tucked into the basket. The candy had been the only gifts they received for Christmas that year.

Despite his busy hours at the bank, after work, Dennis, and sometimes Leon, trekked through the cold, going house to house around the neighborhood collecting canned goods for the baskets. They delivered the cans to the food pantry and helped with sorting. At times, the workers fellowshipped, and other times they worked in companionable silence. It fed a need in Dennis's soul that he never expected.

One night, when sorting canned goods at the church, Dennis discovered that the pastor of Myrna's church was the same man who led Kay's funeral service. Pastor Gary Wright was exactly the way Dennis remembered him. He was kind and caring with a huge heart bent toward serving others. He was the reason Myrna learned that Kay had passed away. After visiting Dennis, Pastor Wright had stopped next door at Myrna's house to ensure that she knew about what her devastated neighbor was facing, seemingly alone if the pastor's intuition was correct. The pastor was a friend of Myrna and knew that she possessed a tender, compassionate heart and would look after the young man as best as he would let her.

As Dennis got to know Pastor Gary while sorting the donations, his passion for helping others inspired Dennis to view the world beside himself differently. Pastor Gary kept his eyes open and his mind engaged in what was happening around him. As a result, he found creative ways to meet needs and was an encouragement to both his church flock and those in the neighborhood surrounding it. Pastor Gary talked a lot about the ministries the church had for the community, and how some of their most important programs happened at Christmas when many folks struggled for all sorts of reasons.

Dennis found himself wanting to live the way Pastor Gary did. The pastor's inspiration led him to help with yard work and odd jobs for widows like Myrna and to join the crew building the set for the church Christmas pageant. Dennis had never seen a Christmas play before, but the past few months had been full of new experiences, and doing something meaningful was much better than sitting on his couch night after night.

On Friday, December 23, the shepherds, wise men, and other cast members lined up to share the sacred story with the congregation. Dennis sat with Myrna, Leon, and Essie Mae. As they waited for the play to begin, Dennis was proud to point out his handiwork on the set pieces he built. He smiled when tiny cast members filed on stage in their ancient dress. The children sang and told about God's own son coming to earth to redeem the creation that had turned from Him. As Dennis listened, his mind was in awe of this kind of love. The message was like none other he had ever heard of before. It was as Myrna had told him; forgiveness was available to all. Dennis felt a yearning for his soul to be made right with his maker. Could be that he had always felt such a longing but never knew where or how he could find contentment.

He waited around afterward to speak to Pastor Gary. The pastor kindly explained the truth of Christ's birth, his life and purpose, and the impact of his death and resurrection to Dennis. He was amazed to learn that the steps towards redemption and peace with God were laid out in His holy Bible and that God's salvation was available to anyone. A person had to decide if they would choose to believe and accept the free salvation God offered. Dennis felt hopeful. For the first time in his life, he had clear direction on the path he could take. When Pastor Gary asked him if he wanted to put his faith in Christ as his redeemer, Dennis replied, "Yes!"

After the play, Dennis, Essie Mae, and Leon went over to Myrna's house for a slice of pound cake and a cup of coffee. They talked about the Davis and Kuntz family Christmas traditions. Dennis had never heard of many of them due to his parents never making much of an effort to celebrate the holiday. Pop had said it was a bunch of bunk for weak-willed people. Mom and Dennis' siblings had not wanted to oppose Pop, so on Christmas, the Oswalds carried on as normal, while other families were having a merry time. He and Kay had exchanged gifts but neither had understood the true meaning or background of the holiday. Essie Mae told them that one of her favorite Christmas traditions was the gathering together of her whole family. Tomorrow, Essie Mae and Leon's brother would come pick them up so they could spend Christmas and a few more days at the farmstead. Both siblings were excited at the prospect of spending time at home with their family.

"Myrna and Dennis, I asked Mama and Daddy if it would be all right, and they were ecstatic about the idea. They want to meet you both. We wondered if you might join us for Christmas Day lunch, if you want to drive up that morning and head back at dusk. The farm is a little under a two hour drive. If you would consider it, the whole family would be thrilled to have you out. The boys will want to show you city folks all about farming and their animals. Not much crop to look at except what we have put up from the harvest. I suspect you might find it interesting, if nothing else, and the food will be good. My mama and all the ladies are wonderful cooks. So what do you say?" Essie Mae issued the invitation sweetly.

Dennis was surprised but pleased by the thought of having somewhere to go for the holiday. Especially now that it meant something special to him for the first time since he was a kid who had hoped that the Santa Claus he heard of would think him good enough for a present on Christmas morning. He was curious about farm life too. He had never been to a real farm before, unless a body counted those that the soldiers walked through on their marches from one camp or battlefield to the next in Korea.

Myrna was smiling too. "What do you think, Dennis? Should we show those farmers how we city folk celebrate Christmas?" He nodded and it was settled. They would drive to the homestead on Christmas morning.

With shining eyes, Essie Mae told them she had other exciting news to report. Dennis's bank had called offering a position in the accounting department. She had accepted the job yesterday and would start the first week of the New Year. This job paid much better and meant no extra shifts at Frank's. Myrna cheered and Dennis sent Essie Mae a big smile.

Then Myrna said she would be right back. She shuffled down the hall and returned with three packages wrapped in brown paper. "I could have saved these for Christmas now that we will be together, but I think it will be nice to open them with just the four of us."

Myrna handed each of them a package. Leon opened a bright blue scarf. He rubbed it against his cheek. "Soft, pretty. Thank you!"

Essie Mae received warm knit mittens. "Double layered to keep out the cold," Myrna said with pride. Essie oohed and aahed over the soft rose color and luxurious warmth.

Dennis's package held a Bible. "I had a sense you would be needing one." He could not believe the timing. His throat was tight as he thanked Myrna.

Essie Mae and Leon also brought presents they had stowed in a bag. To Myrna they gave a silver heart-shaped broach. "Because you give your heart so freely and love with all of it," Essie Mae told her with tears in her eyes. The women hugged and Leon circled his arms around them both.

Next, Essie Mae looked bashfully at Dennis and handed him a long, narrow box. Inside, a fine-looking pen was nestled among tissue paper. "It's the nicest pen I have ever owned. Thank you," he told them sincerely.

The ladies began to pick up the wrapping paper when Dennis asked them to wait because he too had gifts. Dennis hurried to his home next door, glad he had spent time last Saturday picking out special items for each of his friends.

To Leon, he gave a music box. Leon loved winding Myrna's music box and hearing it play its sunny little tune.

Myrna received a lovely wrist watch. Dennis noticed that she often left the room to check her kitchen clock. He had never seen her wear a watch and figured she did not have one at the present. "Very dainty and feminine. I appreciate it, son!" She turned it this way and that admiring the glitzy timepiece.

Dennis had walked around the store for a while trying to find something just right for Essie Mae. Finally, he'd found it. He had observed how she often covered her hair with a cotton scarf when walking outside in the cooler weather. The scarf was a drab color, but he heard her telling Myrna it had been on clearance at the five and dime. Dennis thought Essie Mae should have something beautiful to wear. He had purchased a royal blue, green, gray, and white floral wool scarf. It enhanced her coloring and the gray green leaves matched her eyes. Essie Mae and Myrna both gushed over it.

When they all began to yawn, Dennis saw Essie Mae and Leon home. They walked close together bracing against the icy wind that had picked up in the past hours. As they reached the door, Dennis handed Essie Mae her packages while Leon headed inside. Softly, Essie Mae said, "Dennis, thank you again for my beautiful scarf. And thank you for putting my résumé in for the job. I...well it's been good to get to know you. I'll see you on Christmas." With that, she stood on her tiptoes and brushed a soft kiss to his cheek and went inside.

Dennis stood looking at the closed door until the cold began to sink into his bones. *What a night!* he thought as he turned toward home.

Dennis was awake by five o'clock on Christmas morning. He and Myrna attended the Christmas Eve service last night, but here he lay wide awake. He stayed in bed for a while with no real reason to get up quite yet since he and Myrna planned to leave at eight. The Kuntz family would be going to church that morning, so Dennis figured they did not want to arrive before their hosts were home.

Dennis was interested in the idea of going to a farm. It was a whole other way of life that he had never had much cause to think about. He was curious to meet Essie Mae and Leon's family as well. Each member had been described in bits and pieces throughout the past few months. From what Dennis gathered, the family was close-knit and worked hard to make a life together.

Myrna was ready right on time and had managed to bake a pie to bring along. Dennis had thought hard about his contribution to the day and settled on bringing some Dr. Pepper for everyone. His cooking was still in its infancy and he would readily admit that he had a fifty percent success rate of the food tasting good. He figured that most people would find the soda an acceptable offering from a bachelor. It felt strange to think of himself as one despite the fact that he and Kay had only been married a little over a year. Dennis shook his head at the thought. Today was Christmas Day. He wanted to enjoy the day with the Kuntz family for what it was instead of reliving the same reel of his regrets and failures.

Ten minutes later, they left the skyline of Fort Worth behind them heading west and a little bit north. Rolling hills with scrub brush trees and cattle dotted the landscape. Dennis and Myrna enjoyed a companionable silence for the most part. Occasionally, one or the other would share an observation or story. The big, wide city thoroughfares turned into small farm to market roads, finally leading to the gravel farm lane. At the end of the drive stood a sprawling, ranch style house, a barn, and a few out buildings, all of which looked old but in good repair. The owners' hard work and attention to detail was clear.

As Dennis pulled his car next to a truck and another car already parked near the barn, people began to spill out of the home. Dennis's eyes found Essie Mae first, and then lit on an older woman who had the same light brown hair, but streaked through with silver. Her face was kind and welcoming, as was that of the ox of a man who stood beside her. The way Essie Mae told it, her father appeared imposing, but was known for his generosity and willingness to lend a hand to a neighbor in need. Essie Mae had also warned them of his quick wit and love for a good practical joke. "You'd better stay on your toes when papa is around," she had advised the other night.

Beside Essie Mae and Leon's parents were a smattering of young people and children. Two of the women looked nearly identical; Dennis figured they were the younger sisters who fell between Essie Mae and Leon in birth order. That left the other woman to be her brother Louis's wife, with Louis standing beside her, assessing him with interest. The other men next to her sisters must be the brother-in-laws, Dennis assumed. He knew the Kuntz had lost their oldest son, Warren, in the North African campaign in early 1943. For the children, there was a set of twin girls with matching braids, three boys of varying ages, and a baby on every mother's hip.

Dennis climbed out of the car and realized Essie Mae's dad had a slight but noticeable limp as he made his way toward them. "Howdy, y'all! Merry Christmas! We have heard so much about you and welcome you to our home. I am Alden Kuntz and this here is my wife, Francis, and our children and grandchildren. This group may look like a lot to you all, but there will be fifteen more joining us before the day is through. Most will come in the evening though, so you don't have to worry about there not being enough food." With that promise, Alden gave a hearty laugh.

Carefully, he clasped Myrna in a gentle hug and then looked to Dennis and hesitated, taking his measure. Dennis figured he must have passed inspection, because he found himself enveloped in the first hug a grown man had given him in over twenty-five years.

Dennis felt off balance for a moment, but then smiled at his host. The older man seemed pleased by the sincerity of his gesture. Louis and his wife Anna introduced themselves and their brood: two of the boys, the twins, and a baby. Next, Caron and her husband Travis gave their baby and young boy's names. The last group consisted of the youngest sister, Penny, and her husband Aaron and their baby girl. It was a good-looking, lively bunch. They ushered Myrna and Dennis inside thanking them for the pie and Dr. Pepper.

The women headed off to the kitchen to continue their preparations, asking Myrna to join them as they went. There was still an hour or so before the special Christmas lunch would be ready. The men offered to take Dennis around the farm.

As they walked past fields and grazing livestock, Dennis was told the story of how Alden's great-grandfather, Victor Kuntz, and his young family came to Texas from Germany in the late 1870's. First, he tried his hand at ranching, but decided the trail life was not for him, especially as the railroad moved west and fencing went up, blocking the easy paths to market. The men pointed to far off fields and pastures and shared about the crops and the animals they raised. Louis's home was near the backfields of the property, giving his family some autonomy while sharing the homestead's workload.

Essie Mae's brother-in-laws also told a bit about their background. Aaron was a banker and worked for his uncle's bank in Graham. He and Dennis exchanged shop talk for a few minutes. The couple lived in town, though Aaron admitted that he missed the wide open spaces like the Kuntz's farm and the one he grew up on.

Travis was the most reserved man of group. Dennis could not get a good read on the man. In a family of bighearted people, he was noticeably standoffish. Travis only offered that he worked in town as a lawyer. It could be that due to his law practice, he experienced the uglier side to people and was hesitant to trust an outsider too quickly. Dennis knew there was no sense in letting the man's behavior bother him. After the tour, the men headed inside to see what the women needed them to help with.

Dennis found Myrna and Essie Mae in the center of the kitchen. Myrna sat at the table talking with Mrs. Kuntz, who was mashing potatoes. Essie Mae was at the sink washing dishes with her sisters. They were laughing, but an undercurrent of strain could be detected by the hard edge to Essie Mae's cheeks and the proud angle of Caron's jaw. Dennis would have to remember to ask her later about her sisters.

Now that he thought on it, Essie Mae rarely spoke of Caron and had mentioned Penny only a time or two. He only had one sister but recollected all the drama between Janet and her friends. Seemed that they would have loud disagreements and one would stomp out of the house. Maybe having three females so close together in age could be the cause of the tension. Could be that Dennis read the situation incorrectly. Whatever the case with the sisters may be, Anna, he had heard much about. It was clear based on their interactions that Anna and Essie Mae had been good friends long before they were family.

He glanced back to Myrna once again. She was watching the same scene he had been until she looked his way and sent him a nod that communicated much with nary a spoken word.

Leon came into the kitchen with red cheeks from being out in the wind while tramping around the farm with the rest of the men. His mother put an arm around him and pulled him close. Dennis had never seen Leon with such a glow about him, not even the times they played checkers and ate his favorite treats. It was obvious that if he had a choice, he would disregard the doctor's advice and live at home instead of in the tiny, city house.

Mrs. Kuntz announced it was time to eat. From the oldest to the youngest, a hush descended as Mr. Kuntz thanked the Lord for each person present and blessed the food. Dennis was deeply moved by the simple and sincere prayer. After the "amen," the serving line was opened for the ladies first and then the gentlemen. Roasted turkey, honey ham, deviled eggs, rolls, and casseroles of all kinds were loaded onto waiting plates. The tantalizing aromas urged him to try a little scoop of everything. Louis nodded his approval at Dennis's mounded plate and invited him to sit to his right. The meal was everything Essie Mae promised and then some.

Later, the kids ran around showing off new toys and banging on the piano. Aunts, uncles, cousins, and Oma Leonie joined the Kuntzes as they day progressed. In the afternoon, the whole group gathered around the piano and sang Christmas carols and listened to the holy story of Christ's birth. By the end of the day, Dennis and Myrna left for home full of good food and with new friends.

Myrna dozed on the drive back to Fort Worth. Dennis could tell that she had enjoyed herself but was not used to being out and busy for such an extended period of time. The stars twinkled in the sky above them by the time they pulled onto their street.

Dennis helped Myrna to her door.

"Dennis, this has been one of the best Christmases I have spent in a while. It would not have been the same without you."

"Thank you, Myrna. It's been a real blessing to know you too," Dennis replied with all sincerity.

Afterward, as he sat listening to the radio, the popular song "White Christmas" from the film of the same name, played across the air waves. It had not been a white Christmas this year nor was snow on Christmas common in Fort Worth, but it had been ideal for him. He enjoyed seeing the Kuntz family spend time together. Even the sisters, who had seemed at odds earlier, had put their differences aside to celebrate and take pleasure in each other's company. Dennis was glad that he had been invited.

A thought that had been niggling at his brain for a while began to persist in its insistence to be acknowledged. Watching the Kuntz family had made Dennis wrestle again with the idea of seeking out his own father. He did not expect things to go as easily between them as with the Kuntzes, but maybe he could show Pop a little of the grace he was learning about.

After work on December 27, Dennis checked the mail. He had received his usual Christmas card from Janet, his only sister. Janet apologized for the belated note saying that a month earlier she and her husband welcomed a sweet baby boy whom they named Ronald after their favorite motion picture star, Ronald Reagan. Her husband, Bill, had met the famous star when Reagan had been forced to flee from a mob of fans and hide in the airport's employee lounge. Bill had been eating lunch there at the time and enjoyed talking with the man so much he asked if Janet would not mind naming their child Ronald, if it was a boy. "That Ronald Reagan is going to be someone great, Janet. I want our boy to have a strong name," Janet wrote, quoting Bill's words in her note.

Her card also included a snapshot of a handsome baby with a dark swatch of thick, black hair much like Dennis's own hair. Janet explained that she had not wanted to share the blissful news of her pregnancy in the condolence card she sent after learning of Kay's passing. She hoped that one day her little family would make it back to Texas for a visit and Dennis could meet his nephew and brother-in-law. Janet also told Dennis to let her know if he ever planned to come out to California. He was welcome to their living room sofa bed anytime. She thought that Dennis and Bill would get along real well. Bill was an Air Force veteran and now worked in the radar tower at their local airport.

Dennis could sense Janet's happiness in this latest letter. He was glad that his sister's life was stable now—no, thriving was more accurate. It was good to see that one of his siblings had done well.

He thought about Terry. Dennis knew he should write his brother soon. He had seen firsthand what a difference it could make in one's life when someone made the effort to take the initial hard step and reach out. He would think on it a bit. Finding the right words would be difficult, in part due to not seeing his brother in over five years and considering that he was in prison.

For now, Dennis felt it was time to write Janet a real letter for a change. So many times he had answered her card with a short note of his own, nothing more. Two years ago, he mentioned his marriage to Kay in Janet's birthday card that year as if it was nothing special. He had barely dashed off a note to her about Kay's death, instead sending a copy of the obituary as notice, which he had stuffed into the envelope with a paper that briefly read, "I love you.

Kay passed away in an accident a month ago," with his signature at the bottom.

Dennis sat down at the small dinette table with a few pieces of paper and an addressed envelope.

Dear Janet,

I was happy to receive your Christmas card and picture of baby Ronald. He is a strong looking little guy. You did well, kid! I appreciate you always keeping up with me and your kind words about Kay's death. I am doing a little better now. I have made a few friends with some neighbors and some guys at work. They are helping me talk about the accident and come to peace with Kay being gone. It's actually a bit more complicated than that, but I will save that story for another time. Know though, that for the first time in a long while, I think I am going to be okay. I don't know when I can come out for a visit. I have some debts to pay off first, but I hope to make it out to you some day. For now, I would like to hear your voice some time. I do not have a telephone at my rental house but my friend Martin said I could use his. I know long distance calls aren't cheap; you can reverse the charges to me. If this is agreeable to you, let's plan for a Sunday afternoon soon. I look forward to hearing from you.

Love, Dennis

Dennis was satisfied with his letter and put it to the side to send out in the morning. He still felt restless when thinking about his family. He had no idea how to begin the search for his mother, or if he wanted to. Part of him was curious about what had happened to her, but the other side could not bear to know. It had been twelve years since she left. She might no longer be living. He decided to save his thoughts on his mom for another day.

For now, he recognized that the time had come to reach out to his father. When he arrived back in Fort Worth after Korea, he'd gone to the house his family had been renting last he knew of to see if Pop was still there. Mrs. Wilson from next door had told him Pop had moved out a year earlier around the time Terry was sent to prison. She'd thought he ended up a few blocks away at somewhere called The Oaks Apartments.

At that time, Dennis had no intention of seeing the old man but wanted to know his whereabouts so he could settle in a different neighborhood. He'd had no interest in running into his pop out on the street or at the grocery store. Tomorrow, he would find out where Pop hung his hat these days. *More like stashed his liquor,* he thought bitterly before reminding himself that dwelling on such thoughts would not help him make peace with his father. He would visit Pop and see where things led from there. Dennis had learned that with Pop, it was best not to have any expectations.

Dennis's search discovered The Oaks Apartments still stood. He decided to go see if Pop lived there after lunch on Saturday. He tried to fight off his nerves all week by busying himself at work. Due to the Christmas and New Year's holidays, many employees had taken time off, so he had plenty to keep himself occupied with. Dennis worked up until the bank closed its doors to celebrate New Year's. He had been invited to a fellow employee's house for a party to ring in 1956, but had begged off saying that it was one of Kay's favorite holidays and he felt it best to stay home this year. Dennis was not ready to reveal to anyone that he would visit his father that afternoon. If the visit went poorly, he would need time to decompress away from the eyes of others. He also meant what he said about spending the evening reflecting on the holiday Kay had loved so much.

Around one o'clock in the afternoon, Dennis pulled up to and parked at the crumbling curb in front of a rundown, dingy apartment building. It was a dreary looking place with paint peeling off the crooked shutters and the red brick scarred from grime and the weather's wear and tear. The front lawn was primarily large patches of dirt with sparse scraps of dead grass every so often. Winter was always a harsh season to see a place. Could be that it was a nice building in the other seasons, but Dennis thought that unlikely. He entered the central door of the apartment building and checked the mail slots until he found one labeled Oswald. Apartment 2E was about to receive a visitor.

Dennis rehearsed what he planned to say as he took the stairs to the second floor. He paused in front of 2E, then knocked with all the courage he could muster. No answer came from within, but he heard enough noise to know the apartment was occupied. He knocked again.

"Who is it?" came the familiar rough tone of his father's voice.

Dennis pushed down the nerves that had been building all day. He swallowed then cleared his throat. "Dennis, sir." Pop had always insisted upon his kids and wife showing him respect. Too bad he did not share the same deference toward them.

The door opened a sliver. "What do you want? Money? Too bad! I ain't got any more than what you kids bled from me years ago."

"Sir, I am here to see you and find out how you are," Dennis replied evenly while trying to peer into the darkened room behind his dad.

175

"You want to see me, huh?" Pop let out a belch of a laugh and opened the door a slight bit wider. "Here I am, kid."

He looked awful. His skin and eyes were tinged with a yellowish hue but also spotted with some sort of red rash too. His bones protruded from under the clothing that hung limply on his once robust form. Pop was dressed in the same haphazard manner as Dennis had last seen him. His t-shirt was more brown than white from sweat and filth. His navy pajama shorts were wrinkled so deeply they looked like they had been pressed that way intentionally.

"May I come in?" Dennis asked politely, trying to keep his horror and pity from being revealed in his tone.

"Not on your life, boy. I done raised you to manhood. What more do you want with me?" Pop growled back, his lips and yellowed teeth formed into the same familiar snarl Dennis remembered.

"Pop, I am here because you are my father. I care about you."

"I see that the Army made you soft. Look, I didn't ask you to care, but you will be happy to know that your old man is finally getting what's coming to him. Doctor says my liver is on borrowed time. Too much alcohol he says. What does he know?" Pop asked the rhetorical question then took a big swig of something from a brown glass bottle. Gin, if Dennis's nose proved correct.

"Pop, I'm sorry. I don't want you to die. I'm here now. What can I do to help you?" Dennis's well-meaning words sent Pop into a rage. His face mottled red and he raised the bottle menacingly.

"Get out of here. I don't want you. I never did. You kids were all your worthless mother's idea." He lost his breath at the exertion, then caught it long enough to slam the door in Dennis's stunned face. The dead bolt locked with a heavy click. Dennis could hear his father's cough rattle through the thin apartment door.

A neighbor peeked her head out from her own door. In a heavy Polish accent, she explained to him that Paul Oswald was an ill man. Dennis told her he knew this, but the man was his father, and he wanted to help him.

"You leave me your number. I call when there is news or maybe you can visit when he feel good and is in a much better mood," she said kindly.

Dennis wrote Martin's telephone number on the scrap paper she handed him and explained that these friends could take a message or contact him if she called. He thanked her and headed toward home. The visit had gone about how he had expected but not how he'd hoped. Was it too late for him and Pop to reconcile? Did he honestly even want to forgive the man who had hurt him so deeply? Maybe he was a sucker or more of an optimist that he thought, but yes, he wanted a relationship with his father.

In the mean-time, Dennis let his mind anesthetize itself from Pop's cruel words. It was a trick Miles had taught him around the time he was five and Miles was eight. "Don't let Pop's words sting you, Dennis. You don't want to be mad all the time like he is. You got to think about happy things or you'll get mean like Pop," Miles had warned. Whether Pop meant his words or not, Dennis would not waste his time thinking about it. He had to focus on what his heavenly father thought about him instead of the angry ravings of his broken earthly father.

As he sat at home on New Year's Eve, Dennis reminisced on how Kay loved the holiday's parties. She had delighted in the splendor and excitement of parties in general, but especially New Year's, waxing poetic and saying it made everything fresh and full of grand possibilities.

He even went to search for the photograph a friend of Kay's took of the two of them on the date two years earlier. They had gone to one of her Montgomery Ward friend's home to celebrate. In the picture, they wore shiny, triangular party hats and had paper horns in their mouths. He smiled remembering how they had laughed and reveled in the joy of being together and in love.

The memories were bittersweet. It no longer stung when he thought of Kay; there was just an ache from knowing she was gone forever. He missed her, but he could finally accept he was still on this earth for a reason, and so he must go on living the best he could. In his heart, he believed Kay would have done the same had their places been switched.

It did not mean that he was ready to ask Essie Mae on a date though. Dennis was not sure how to handle that situation. It felt like he was in middle school, saying he liked her. He did though. But like a kid, he needed some time to mature—to grow into who he was coming to be.

Though he was exhausted by ten o'clock, Dennis forced himself to stay up until midnight. It was Kay's tradition, and he wanted to honor it one last time, because when the timing was right, he hoped to start new traditions with a woman who had come into his life at a dark point and had not shied away. A woman who saw the harsh realities of life and chose to face them with strength and joy.

Chapter 13

December 1955

Winter in north Texas was a funny thing. One day a person was soaking up Vitamin D on a sixty degree day full of sunshine and not a cloud in sight. The following day, a cold front rolled through in a matter of hours and out came the heavy coat, scarf, and mittens. Christine compared the weather pattern to her personal life.

At times, people were warm and kind to her until they remembered her misdeed. It was not everyone, but Christine was tired of the reproach, except from Dr. Alan Evans. His moods were just as tempestuous, but Christine did not mind when he gave her the cold shoulder. He never said a word about that night at the theater, to which she was relieved. What could she say that would not make for an uncomfortable work environment? She and Margaret reasoned that he did not like to be alone in a new city or that he was hoping to be a heartbreaker with the way he went through his rolodex. Christine gave him wide berth either way. She had experienced enough heartache to last her a lifetime.

Christine also perceived her own attitude to vacillate like the December weather. At times, she welcomed Sheila's visit and the clarity she hoped it would bring, but as the hours ticked down, she became more nervous that Sheila would claim Pete as her own. Day after day, Christine carefully thought over her feelings and reactions to any news she could imagine Sheila sharing. When the time came, she wanted to be prepared and support Sheila in the same manner that her friend had cared for her through the years.

On Tuesday, the sixth of December, Pete announced that the night program would take a three week break following next weeks' class. The church fellowship hall was hosting a dinner one week, the scenes and costumes for the Christmas Eve play would fill the room the week after that, and then the church would have limited hours due to the New Year holiday.

At the final Tuesday meeting of the year, all of the instructors held a party for any student past or present to attend. They played games incorporating Christmas themes and practiced some of the concepts that had been taught throughout the year. On behalf of the volunteers, John gave each student a pad of paper and a pencil as a present. To Christine, it had seemed like a simplistic gift, yet the gratitude that shone on many of the faces around the room reminded Christine that meeting people's needs was better than giving them something fancy but useless. A glass paperweight or tie pin was meaningless when what one needed was a way to practice English or write a letter to a loved one.

Several students also brought small tokens for their teachers. Christine received an orange, a crochet doily, and a hand drawn sketch of a petunia. Each gift was a beautiful and thoughtful offering. Christine gave her students delicious caramel candies wrapped in shiny paper. She enjoyed seeing their faces as they tried a piece of the creamy sweet. For some, it was their first caramel ever.

At the end of the night when all had been picked up and set right again, Christine wished Dave, Dolores, John, and Joe a Merry Christmas and happy New Year. She attended another congregation and would participate in her own church's festivities, not seeing them until the classes resumed in January.

Dolores hugged Christine and told her it was a delight to have Christine teach with them and a joy to see her open her heart toward others and help them succeed. It touched Christine to know that the other volunteers could see that she was developing and making an impact in the students' lives.

Christine and Pete were the last to leave. Although the others seemed to gather their materials and gifts quickly, Christine knew she was lingering, hoping to have a few minutes alone with Pete when they walked out. It could be her last time with him before knowing he was taken.

Pete smiled down at her and took the box of supplies and gifts she carried. "Christine, this fall I was not sure if you would join our program. Not that I blamed you. You have had to handle and persevere through difficulties that many people will never deal with in their lifetime. You have done so with grace." He shuffled his feet.

Christine leaned forward subconsciously, waiting for his next words. Instead, another male voice spoke.

Pastor Schaefer called to them again from across the lawn from the parsonage. "Sorry I am late getting over. Pam's mother called about her Christmas travel plans. She's coming in from Cincinnati. Let me get that key from you and let you folks get out of the cold."

The pastor thanked them both for serving their community. He shared that the church had received a call and a number of letters about how thankful each person was for the program. Christine beamed at Pete. She could tell he was pleased by the praise. The two talked with the pastor a minute more before a sudden, chilly drizzle began to beat down on them.

A cheerful "Merry Christmas" was exchanged quickly as they hurried to get out of the rain.

Christine was disappointed that she did not get to hear what else Pete had to say. Perhaps, it was best until she talked to Sheila. The next nine days could not pass soon enough!

The Hinkle family loved to celebrate Christmas. For them, the holy season began the first week of December. They started with the celebration of Advent to focus their hearts and minds on the true reason they celebrated. Over the years, Mom also incorporated the custom of making the traditional sticky buns of her Swedish ancestors in addition to baking dozens of cookies to give away to neighbors and friends. As in their childhood days, Alice and Christine helped frost cookies and pack them in tins for delivery after school and work.

Dad, Mom, Alice, and Christine went out to locate the perfect Christmas tree and spent one Saturday afternoon decking it with all the ornaments and trimmings the poor thing could possibly hold. That evening, her siblings and their spouses and Michael came over to string popcorn and pull taffy. Each day the home was filled with the essence of freshly baked cookies mixed with the rich pine scent of the fir tree they brought home.

At night, her family sat together and sang along to Christmas songs and carols played on the record player. It really was a special time, as if they all sensed that there would never again be a Christmas season quite like it in the future. Christine went to bed tired after each full day, but never forgot to say a prayer for Dennis Oswald. She guessed he might miss his wife a lot at this time of year. As she prayed for peace for him, she also prayed it for herself.

Sheila Grant arrived several days before Christmas. In true fashion, she practically ran off the train and gave Christine, Patty, and her father enthusiastic hugs. Mr. Grant was a quiet, unassuming man who took the bit of pandemonium from his boisterous daughter in stride with a cheerful lilt to his lips. The three young women packed in the back seat of the Grants' car and rode back to Sheila's childhood home. Mrs. Grant gave each of them a tender hug and then handed them thick slices of warm banana bread with pads of butter and a glass of milk to wash it down.

"You girls enjoy." She looked at them all contentedly. "Sure is good to have you all back in this kitchen." She stayed to inquire after Patty and Christine's families before saying, "Oh, Sheila, Daniel and Phyllis arrive tonight with the little ones. We need to be at the train station by five thirty this evening."

"With two of us up north and Glenn in the service, I wonder if my folks will stay here," Sheila mused after her mother left the room. "Daniel says he moved to 'experience a place with real seasons.'"

"Are you planning on staying in Chicago?" Patty asked with a glance at Christine. When they'd had lunch at Patty's house recently, Patty had point blank asked Christine what she thought about Pete. She said that she had noticed the way Christine mentioned him often and that her eyes seemed to take on a sparkle as she spoke about him. Christine hadn't been able to hold back from her best friend and had shared her feelings and anxiety about the nature of Pete and Sheila's relationship. Patty had offered to put out feelers with Nelson, but Christine had dissuaded her to avoid embarrassment.

Now, she waited, anticipating what Sheila would say.

Sheila looked toward the kitchen door before answering. Then she leaned in with a conspiratorial look and whispered, "Gals, I have been offered my dream laboratory research job through a partnership between the university and the hospital and there's a man to boot! I won't bore y'all with all the details just now." Sheila said nodding her head pointedly to the living room where her mother folded laundry. "I plan to talk with my parents later tonight, then I'll tell you all there is to know." Sheila's eyes twinkled with merriment.

"Let's not talk about me, I want to hear all about you both. Give me the juicy details no one ever includes in their letters. Patty, how's it going being married to our homecoming king? Christine, are you enjoying working with Pete? He mentions you at least a few times in every letter." There was good humor in Sheila's tone.

Patty sent Christine the look, urging her to speak up, to ask the question that had imprinted itself on her mind because she went over it so often. Christine said nothing. This was her moment to pose the question. Yet, her lips refused to open. She was too afraid to start a conversation that could put an end to her hopes and wishes. At Christine's hesitation, Patty answered, "Nelson is wonderful, just as one would expect of homecoming royalty. His years at the University of Mississippi really honed all his noble, gentlemanly aspects." They giggled.

Christine knew her chance to ask was now. She dreaded the possibility that Sheila's man was Pete, but surely her old friend would not bait her by mentioning the letters if it were so.

"Out with it, Christine," Sheila said interrupting her thoughts. "I can always tell when you have something on your mind. This one must be a doozy if that look on your face is any indication." Sheila listened as she posed the question that had nagged her for months.

Christine spent Christmas Day spent with her family. After the morning church service, all of her siblings came over for ham, mashed potatoes, collard greens, fried okra, several pies, and the last of the Christmas cookies. They exchanged gifts and watched Michael romp around with Harry in the mound of wrapping paper. Elizabeth announced that she was expecting and would be due in late May. The joyful announcement brought squeals from the women and grins from the men. This time next year, there would be three little ones playing under the tree.

It had been a good day, Christine thought that evening. She reveled in how typical the day had seemed. It had passed so alike to the holy day the year prior. With the exception of a phone call from Bryan, not that the brief five minute telephone call had really had much impact on her day. In fact, most of that call had included a relay of detailed instructions from his mother concerning their New Year's Eve plans. It almost felt nice to be free of the headache and obligations it had caused.

This year, it could be due to the busyness of work or the holiday celebration, but not once had the guilt that was her companion so often of late crossed her mind. She had prayed for Dennis Oswald but not been consumed by the weight of what she had taken from him. Should she feel guilty that she had not obsessed over the accident in a few weeks? Her mind spiraled downward for a moment worrying about the possibility of it all, before she caught herself. Christine realized that she could sit here letting herself experience the guilt because her mind told her she should. It was almost rote at this point. However, another better option was before her. She could choose to let go of her guilt and not plague herself continuously with the unchanging fact that Kay would not spend Christmas with Dennis this year or any of the following. Christine willed herself to accept that she could—no, had to—move on.

New Year's Eve was on a Saturday this year. Christine slept in late, then enjoyed a leisurely breakfast with her family. She ran errands the rest of the morning, taking her time to savor the crisp air and simple pleasure of checking a task off her list. Last year, Christine had spent the day rushing to complete the checklist of "necessary" preparations Mrs. Wharton had given her. This year, there was no pressure to be impeccably dressed and ready for a long night of social obligations and perfect behavior.

Dancing the night away was the only part of that evening Christine found herself missing. Bryan was a superb dancer, light on his feet and a natural leader. He had been fun to partner with on the dance floor. Christine might have enjoyed the envious looks more than one woman sent her way while he twirled her around the ballroom. Being a great dancer was not the equivalent of being a good husband. After nine months, Christine had come to fully accept that she and Bryan were never meant for something more, and to force the issue would have led to the surrender of a lifetime of happiness.

Another big step for Christine happened this morning when she informed her parents that she planned to inquire about roommates again and find a place to rent. If she could not find a roommate, she was planning to use the money she had saved while living at home to find a decent, affordable place to live on her own. Dad and Mom had been happy for Christine, telling her how proud they were of her maturity and bravery to keep on pushing ahead. They had never pressured her, but as a young bird knows when to leave the nest, she felt it was time to spread her wings once more.

Christine told her parents she planned to visit two apartment buildings that had been recommended to her. She also shared her idea to go to the park nearby and walk for a bit in the sunshine, saying that she wanted to review the past year and prepare for the coming one. By three o'clock, the afternoon was cool, in the upper forties, but the bright sun and the walk warmed her enough to sit on one of the path's benches.

Christine reflected on the year 1955. It had started with high society events and an always present demand to be faultless with every reaction and in all circumstances. She had been a pretender. It was not her way of life, nor had she truly wanted it to be, even though she had told herself time and time again this way of living and these people would bring her happiness and fulfillment.

She took a deep breath and looked out over the park's barren trees and yellowed grass that awaited warmer weather and spring rains to revive it again. Like her, they anticipated a new season.

The accident had been the genesis of her downfall and of her freedom. Over the months, she could see how her perspective slowly shifted to acknowledge the truth. She would always carry the sorrow of taking Kay Oswald's life, but she could not bear the sole responsibility for the tragedy that happened that night. Some of the culpability lay with Kay herself and her choice to run out into the street without being able to see around the bus. Try as Christine might; she could not restore Dennis's wife to him.

The months of remorse and regret had dragged her under for a time; the waves of despair threatening any happy moment were like Sisyphus rolling his boulder uphill, enduring an eternity of punishment. Christine had recognized it was no way to live. Yet, it had taken a while for her mind to believe that redemption, and peace for her soul, had been freely offered. She knew now that she should humbly accept the undeserved gift and live in the grace it afforded.

Bryan and Mrs. Wharton's embarrassment over Christine's actions had unknowingly given her freedom when he broke her heart. Perhaps, it had not even been her heart but her pride that had shattered. No longer feeling the insatiable need to be on top of the social pyramid, Christine had seen what truly mattered in this world. It was using the time she had been given to help others and make a difference in their lives and in her community. Though the path to get to this point was not one she would have chosen, Christine was grateful for the lessons she had learned through the pain. She was proud of the more resilient, less self-consumed person she was working to become.

"Mind if I join you?" Pete's voice came from a few feet away where he was leaning against a tree, his eyes focused intently on her. His words were reminiscent of the night they saw the movie together last month.

"Of course!" Christine replied trying to reign in her enthusiasm at the simple question. She moved over to make room for him on the bench.

Pete wore light gray wool trousers under a heavy dark gray coat. He appeared to be prepared to stay a while. There was an undertone of tension with him as well. It was abnormal for the usually light-hearted Pete. Christine watched him for a moment, waiting to see if he would reveal what was causing his uncharacteristic, serious mood.

"When I stopped by your parents' house, your mom told me you planned to come here to walk," he started with, answering Christine's unasked question of whether he had just happened by or if he had come to find her. Her heart flipped and sped up. Pete continued on, "Tomorrow it will be 1956, but I could not let this year end without telling you how I feel about you, how much you mean to me, what you have always meant me." He raised his face and met her eyes. She was transfixed, wondering what he would say next. "I have always admired and liked you,

Christine Hinkle. Always." Bravely, he let the words stand unashamed in the air between them.

When her brain processed his meaning, Christine blinked away the tears that had suddenly sprung into her eyes. "I feel the same way about you, Pete," she whispered, her voice hoarse from the emotion behind her words.

Pete grinned the full, radiant smile Christine had come to hold so dear. "I should say it now because I want you to know. I thought you were cute in middle school when you tried to wear your hair like Rita Hayworth."

Christine laughed. "A sad attempt, but I guess I was the talk of seventh grade for a day."

Pete continued, "I praised the good Lord when Mr. Vickers assigned you to be my biology lab partner when Jeff Haynes was out with pneumonia for two weeks. I wasn't even that sad when you got sick on my shoes while dissecting the frog. It gave me a chance to put my arm around you, even it was to take you to the nurse."

"Your poor loafers. I felt terrible about ruining them."

"I thought about you a lot during the war in Korea. Sheila was my assigned pen pal when the church ladies formed the letter exchange program. I was glad because we had been competitors and friends, nothing more, all throughout our school days. She regaled me with stories about Chicago and what university life was like, but her summer letters were my favorite because you were in them. Eventually, she figured out my admiration for you. She attributes it to her clever mind, but most likely I dropped your name one too many times in my return letters."

The immense relief that Christine had felt after her conversation with Sheila days earlier was second to the new elation that bubbled inside her at Pete's confession. His words thrilled her and infused the drab and dry park with a little more color and life.

She has told me many times over the years that I should find you and speak up. I wanted to but heard you were seeing someone by the time I got back from Korea and worked up the nerve to talk to you. Sheila told me in her May letter that you were no longer seeing anyone. I thought it might be good to give you some time to recover from all that happened, but I selfishly prayed that you would not find someone new in the meantime. When I saw you walk down the church aisle to stand in attendance at Nelson and Patty's wedding, I was struck again by your poise and beauty. As we talked at the reception, you were even better than I remembered."

Christine felt her cheeks warm at his compliments. The admiring look in his eyes made her feel like the most beautiful girl in the world.

Pete reached for her hand and cradled it in his own. "Do you remember we danced to 'Unforgettable' that night? It was like my thoughts about you had been put to music. I have been biding my time these last three months, trying to figure out the best time to say something to you. It has seemed like a lifetime of waiting. So here I am speaking up for the thirteen-year-old Pete and the sixteen-year-old Pete but most importantly for the twenty-three year old Pete."

Pete's honest and bold speech made Christine feel more cherished than she could ever remember. The two of them sat on the park bench exchanging stories, thoughts on each other and life, and future dreams until twilight ebbed toward darkness.

He walked her home in the starlight. It was romantic and dreamy being with Pete and knowing that he felt the same way about her and that maybe they would have a future together.

"May I come back at midnight?" Pete questioned.

Christine's eyes widened as big as a record.

Even in the dim lighting, Christine could see a crimson hue had flushed up Pete's neck collar and cheeks. "That didn't sound like what I meant," He stumbled, embarrassed. "I was invited to my boss's house for a party to celebrate the new year, but I plan to slip out early. I thought maybe if you were up celebrating still, I could give you a New Year's kiss. Start the New Year off right. I'll only stay for a minute," he hurried, shuffling his feet.

Christine thought she might burst at the sweet, romantic idea. "I can't think of a better way to bring in the New Year. You can tap on my window." She pointed to it. "I'll warn Alice. On second thought, I may as well tell my parents you might be by for a minute. Harry will bark and wake them if we don't put him back in their room." Christine looked Pete in the eyes, "I look forward to starting this year with you…I'll be waiting." She added with her own audacious smile before going inside.

Chapter 14

January and February 1956

Essie Mae's new job at the bank began the first week of January. Dennis thought it might be a good gesture to ask Essie Mae if she wanted to ride with him while the weather was still less than ideal. He planned to start walking to work occasionally once the days became pleasant, but for now he would continue to drive in each day. He asked Myrna if she thought his offering a ride to Essie Mae was too forward or might hurt her reputation. Dennis would certainly hate to have what was meant as kindness be misinterpreted or harmful.

Myrna told him she thought it was a considerate offer and that it would not offend Essie Mae if he asked her. She reasoned that Dennis could always make sure to tell anyone who might see them come and leave together that it was just two neighbors saving on transportation costs.

Essie Mae told Dennis she was relieved to have him drive her. It would save her time walking to and waiting at the bus stop; and instead of paying the bus fare, she could pay him for some of the gasoline. He thanked her for the offer but told her there was no need.

From then on, Essie Mae rode to and from work with Dennis each day. Besides Kay and later Myrna, it was the most time Dennis had spent alone with a woman since his adolescence. As he had discovered during the time the spent with Myrna and Leon, Essie Mae was easy to talk with and open to sharing her opinions and ideas. He was fascinated by the way Essie Mae thought about and experienced the world. He enjoyed that Essie Mae liked to read all sorts of books. Her repertoire included the classics of Austen and Bronte as well as modern works of London, Fitzgerald, Sinclair, and Steinbeck. Dennis had not read nearly as many books, but found her reflections on them interesting and thought he might pick up one or two from the library for something to do on cold nights. They also discussed current events and politics. He discovered how much he both learned and was challenged by Essie Mae. The car rides were quickly becoming the part of the day that he most looked forward to. He missed their conversations on the weekends.

He and Kay had not spent much time in deep conversation, even on their early dates. They had always gone to a motion picture show, out dancing, or spent time with her friends. Kay had once told him that life was too full of doing to concern oneself with all the hard things that no one really wanted to speak about. In hindsight, Dennis understood Kay's perspective. She had grown up in a tough home where she often had to fulfill the role of a parent. When she got out on her own and had earned a little money, Kay wanted to spend it on things that made her happy and surrounded her with good memories instead of focusing on harsh realities. He wished for the countless time he would have recognized how to balance all their fun with a healthy dose of embracing and dealing with some of life's difficulties instead of sweeping them to the side until they were too big to face without certain failure.

Although he and Essie Mae were not seeing each other officially, Dennis knew that each conversation and supper together at Myrna's bonded their hearts a little more. Still, he felt an inward checkpoint holding him back from sharing his feelings with Essie Mae. His mind had determined it was the honorable thing to grieve Kay an entire year. Dennis could not give Kay anything else in this life, but he wanted to honor her properly.

So he and Essie Mae continued on through January and February. Both of them were advancing in their jobs. On a personal level, Dennis continued to invest in his friendship with Martin and his family. He attended another one of Ricky's basketball games. This time the Paschal Panthers took on their deep-seated rival the Yellow Jackets from Arlington Heights High School, which was located only a few miles away from their own campus. The game had been riveting!

Dennis was also learning to read the Bible and trust the God who he had never bothered to know before. He began attending a Bible study with Martin at his church, although he still preferred to attend Sunday mornings with Myrna, Essie Mae, and Leon and volunteer with Pastor Gary and his crew.

In late January, Dennis had even enlarged his heart and took in the stray dog Leon found hanging around outside the store while he swept the sidewalk one cold day. Leon had brought the scraggly, freezing mutt to Myrna first. She bathed the pup but said that she could not keep up with an energetic young dog at her age. When Dennis and Essie Mae arrived home from work, Leon proudly showed them the clean dog. He was a cute pooch in need of a few good meals. Dennis empathized with the dog, for he too knew what it was like to feel hungry and alone, uncertain of where your next meal would come from, if at all. Essie Mae figured the pup was a collie cattle dog mix of some kind due to his bone structure and speckled black and white fur. His big, brown eyes soulfully stared at Dennis, willing him to take him home forever. Essie Mae cuddled with the pup but worried about taking the dog in too. Leon seemed to like the dog, but Essie Mae was concerned that the care might be too much for her brother to handle when she was not around. She was getting her footing at the bank, but things were still tight, and she wanted to send home as much as she could to help pay off the medical bills.

"Surely a neighbor wants a handsome, intelligent dog to guard their home," Essie Mae reasoned, though Dennis could tell if she could have her way what she wanted to do was wrap the pup in one of Myrna's blankets and carry him home forever. Dennis had little interest in canvassing the whole neighborhood in the chilly weather to find a volunteer willing to take the dog. He had always wanted a dog as a kid and guessed now was as good a time as any to get one. He agreed to adopt the dog and asked Leon if he might help take the pup outside once while Dennis was at work during the day. Leon looked pleased at the possibility. Together, they named him Burt. He was showered with hugs, meaty bones and puppy chow, and belly rubs often. Burt seemed quite happy with his new friends and roommate.

Burt soon became a friend to which Dennis could share his baloney sandwich or his innermost thoughts. Both at one time were preferred by Burt. In the evenings, the pup would curl up on the sofa next to Dennis with his head resting in Dennis's lap. When Dennis spoke, Burt would quirk his head to the side as if he had more than a basic comprehension of what was said. His doggy grin was present at all times, making Dennis feel like the world was a better place than what he observed some days.

On a rare evening in early February when it was just Myrna, Dennis, and Burt, who had an open invitation to Myrna's house, Myrna called Dennis into the kitchen for a slice of apple pie. "What are your plans for the future, Dennis?"

Dennis was surprised by her question. "Well, I can say that my career trajectory at the bank is much better than I anticipated a year ago. With the increase in salary, I am considering fixing up the house a bit if my landlord will allow it. I have also been setting aside money each month to go visit my sister in California someday, and I am still working on helping Pop."

Since New Year's Eve, Dennis had gone back to Pop's apartment twice to check on him. Pop had not answered the door either time, but Dennis had left a few canned goods that he hoped his father would use. Thankfully, Pop's kind neighbor told him his father was still hanging on and encouraged him to keep trying to see his father.

Myrna nodded, "It seems like you are growing in your faith, advancing at work, and learning to look past your pain. I am proud of you, Dennis. Taking the steps toward reconciliation with your father and extending yourself to have a better relationship with your sister and her family is admirable." She hesitated, then she looked him straight in the face, "What are your intentions toward Essie Mae?"

Dennis believed Myrna asked this question with great care. A ways back, she had admitted to hearing him and Kay fight often due to the thin windows and narrow gap between the two houses. He figured she knew how his relationship with Kay had really been.

Myrna's realistic understanding of his and Kay's relationship and background allowed Dennis the freedom to speak his truest thoughts on the matter with her. "I plan to wait a whole year after Kay's death before pursuing Essie Mae. I am saving every penny I have not committed to the other goals so I can rent a bigger house. If the future turns out how I hope and Essie Mae agrees to marry me, I want Leon to have space should he choose to live with us even if we add children to the mix." Dennis tugged at his collar at that thought. He hoped Myrna understood he was not trying to get way ahead of himself.

Kay had had no inclination to have children until years in the future. Dennis had not given the matter much thought after Kay had adamantly stated her opinions. For the first time in his life, Dennis dreamed there would be a child or two one day in the not too distant future. He could envision Essie Mae baking with them in the kitchen and himself teaching the little one how to ride a bicycle and fly a kite. Maybe they would have a child who liked to fish or play basketball like the Krupsky boys or wanted to become a nurse like their sister Annette. Dennis tried not to let his thoughts drift too far in that direction, although it was fun to imagine.

Myrna looked pleased as can be by his announcement. "Course I'll miss y'all as my neighbors, but this old body is still up for visiting."

Dennis hugged her. "You will always be welcome. For now, I've got to get the girl first."

In the days following, two competing thought processes occupied a lot of Dennis's time. How he could honor Kay on the anniversary of her death? Secondly, how did he let Essie Mae know that he cared about her without it seeming like he was the type of guy to move on too quickly?

Guilt tried to gain a foothold once again, plaguing Dennis when he considered asking Essie Mae on a date in a month or so. When Dennis and Essie Mae rode home from work, discussing their day, he felt the rightness of being with her and working toward a goal together. Later, doubts would creep in. How could he be so faithless to Kay's memory? If he would have loved her more or better, would she be sitting in the car beside him? Maybe Kay would have changed her mind and they would have a child by now.

Dennis agonized over the path before him. When would he feel honorable, like his mourning for Kay was complete and it was acceptable to move forward with his life? What happened if he chose what he wanted too prematurely and ended up losing Essie Mae as well? He was not sure he could face such a great loss again.

If Essie Mae noticed how unsettled Dennis had become, she was too polite to comment on it to him. He tried to grin and put on a good front for her.

Questions and solutions churned through his mind, turning over and over, battering his spirit. While he did laundry or chores around the house, he had a running mental dialogue about the subjects. Burt was often the receiver of Dennis's woeful debates. Thankfully, he would sit there with a grin on his face, providing no more feedback than a wag of his tail, but being a willing, listening ear.

Dennis was learning by Myrna's example that just because he felt one way at first did not mean it was how things really were. It just meant that it was his first reaction, not the most accurate. He needed to allow himself time to think about and reason through issues. So, he continued to wrestle with the what, when, and how details of both honoring Kay and loving Essie Mae.

Valentine's Day fell on a Tuesday this year. On the ride to work, Dennis thought Essie Mae looked especially pretty that morning. She had done her hair in some new style. Dennis was not sure what to call the hairdo but it looked nice on her. He thought he should compliment her on her appearance and fell into silence debating about how to go about it. Essie Mae was also quiet on their morning car ride. Could be she sensed his uncertain mood and wanted to allow him peace to think.

In the course of most of their work days, Dennis saw Essie Mae when passing through the lobby or in the staff work room. She was present in both today, but she seemed subdued then too. Could it be that she was expecting a valentine? Possibly from another man? Walter, from client services, had recently asked Dennis about Essie Mae after he had run into them emerging from the car one morning. Dennis honestly told the man, who was known to have a good work ethic and was extremely personable to coworkers and clients alike, that he did not think Essie Mae was seeing anyone. It had hurt a bit to say so, but if he and Essie Mae were ever to be together, he wanted nothing untoward to be between them. He had never shared his feelings, but he could not expect another guy not to see Essie Mae for the wonderful, appealing woman she was. Maybe she had no interest in Dennis and would welcome Walter's pursuit. He would hate to be the one who stood in the way of Essie Mae's happiness. As a result, he spent the day trying to push away his concerns over whether or not Walter or any other unknown contender would reveal his hand today.

The car ride home was almost as silent as the drive in. When Dennis pulled to the curb in front of her house, Essie Mae smiled. "Dennis, would you like to have a piece of pie on the porch with me? The day is pretty mild."

Dennis's eyebrows rose. He was shocked that the day's silence had led to such a question. "Of course, yes." He scrambled to park and open Essie Mae's door for her.

Dennis waited on the small porch stoop while Essie Mae went inside to fetch the slices of pie. She returned with two china plates complete with generous servings of pie and a fork and a glass of milk for each of them.

"Cherry, raspberry?" he questioned examining the pie.

"Yes, after Christmas, Mama sent me home with the last of the canned cherries and raspberries. I have been saving them. I saw how much you enjoyed the pie I made at Thanksgiving; I baked this one fresh last night." She beamed, then put her plate to the side and examined him before continuing. "Dennis, I have appreciated your kindness to Leon and myself. When I first met you this fall, I could tell you were working through a lot of difficult issues, yet you made time to play checkers with Leon and to listen to Myrna while fixing up little things at her house. You helped me get my job at the bank and that has been a huge blessing. I have enjoyed becoming your friend and hope you count me as one too." She paused then, brushing the little wisps of hair away from her face.

He heard her soft inhale. She began speaking again, "Dennis, you have given much to us all. I found myself thinking on it a bit and loving you for your caring spirit. I know you loved Kay and that you need time to grieve her but someday maybe you could think of me as more than a friend, and if not, I am always your friend."

Dennis tried to comprehend what Essie Mae was saying. For the second time that afternoon, Essie Mae had surprised him. His mind spun with all he wanted to say. The words and feelings he'd thought about so much now jumbled in his head.

Finally, Dennis's brain caught up with the present. He loved Essie Mae for her long-suffering ways, her compassion, and her hard work. She was a smart, beautiful woman. He knew in that moment that he could love Essie Mae while still honoring Kay's memory. But he would have to be honest with Essie Mae too. His had not been a loving marriage like her parents'. Though he knew many couples had disagreements, he and Kay's marriage had been broken. There were legitimate reasons behind Kay's choice to leave him, though he believed that if they had talked things through, worked at it, and sought out help from others their future would have been different. He knew he would have to tell Essie Mae the dark truth and let her decide if he was still what she wanted.

"Essie Mae, I have spent the past few weeks trying to figure out and pray about how to tell you that I admire you. Your strength of spirit, the selfless way you take care of Leon and love on Myrna even when you were working two jobs and bone tired has amazed me. I have come to love you too, but I have to be honest with you. The night that Kay was hit was not due to negligence on the part of the driver. Kay was leaving me. She had already packed her bags and stowed them in the trunk of a friend's car. She asked to meet me at Frank's so she could tell me she was leaving me and would be filing for divorce. I want to tell you that I was a poor and innocent victim in all of it, but I wasn't." He searched her face trying to gauge her reaction at his personal indictment.

He breathed out slowly then added further reason for her condemnation. "I fought with her and hurt her feelings more times than I care to count. At times, I would walk out of the room on her if an argument was not going my way. Sometimes I hated her. I was not the husband I should have been or would want to be now that I know better. I know this is a chunk to swallow, but I need you to hear it from me so you know what you are getting. I also want you to understand that I am working on changing. I know Christ now and Martin, Pastor Gary, and Myrna have been studying the Bible with me and answering my questions. I believe that I am maturing and hope to be a better man." He stopped. It was a lot to admit. The truth could be a vile thing, but it was right to expose the depravity of his soul as well as the hope he now experienced. Essie Mae deserved the truth, not some lie that would be easy to feed her but would lead to their destruction in the end.

Essie Mae met his eyes and took his hand in hers. Never before had she been so bold. "I know you have been through so much. I have watched you change from a bitter, angry man to one who gently cares for those he loves. I have seen it with your volunteering at church, your treatment of Myrna, Leon, and myself. You even took in Burt when he could give nothing in return to you. I do not expect you to be perfect, Dennis. Please know that I am not without fault either. The reason Leon and I came to Fort Worth three years ago was in part because Leon really does need to be close to a hospital and also because I was angry at Caron for stealing my beau, Travis, from me." Dennis felt Essie Mae's hand tighten around his. Their intertwined fingers made him believe they were stronger together somehow.

Essie Mae's expression was poignant. "I think I had a crush on Travis Green since I was in the first grade and he was in fifth grade. He was a friend of my brothers and came out to the farm often while we were growing up. His folks lived in Graham proper and the farm was a novelty to him. After he came home from law school, he established a practice in Graham and he began to visit the farm again. Only Warren was gone, and Louis had married and moved further down the lane with Anna. Travis asked me for a walk or to sit out on the porch with him on a few occasions, but it meant more to me than it did to him. Turns out he liked Caron more and they had been meeting up secretly in town on occasion. She is seven years his junior. I was crushed and angry to be passed over for my younger sister. Penny sided with Caron when it all came out in the wash. It felt like I lost two sisters in an instant. The bookkeeping job in Fort Worth seemed like a godsend. Mama and Daddy agreed that it was best for me to have some time away from the daily reminders of Travis and Caron."

Her story surprised him, but it made him understand and care for her even more. Essie Mae was very even tempered and patient with anyone he had seen her interact with, including difficult clients at the bank. He guessed some people might describe him as laid back and levelheaded too. It was ironic. Surely some philosopher had reasoned that ones who were closest to a person could bring out the best and worst in their loved ones. It certainly seemed true based on his, Myrna's, and Essie Mae's stories.

Essie Mae continued, "I will happily face hard times together with you. I am not some simpering southern belle. I have picked cotton until my fingers bled, bound them, and picked some more." Essie Mae stopped then, waiting patiently for his response. She treated Leon this way, always patient, allowing time for him to form the words he wanted to say.

Dennis took his time, getting the words just right in his head before saying, "I didn't want to dishonor Kay in any way by speaking at the wrong time or mislead you with my past being what it was. I guess God has a funny sense of humor and took it out of my hands. You speaking up was the sign I think I needed. Essie Mae, I have lots of ideas about the future and I want to hear yours too, but for now, I would like to start by taking you to dinner."

They both gave a relieved chuckle and ate the forgotten pie. Dennis thought it tasted sweet, but not quite as good as the possibilities that were before him now.

Chapter 15

Winter 1956

Christine's future looked bright these days. She and Pete talked daily, spending many evenings having supper together or going on walks around the neighborhood. Most important, they listened to each other's thoughts, opinions, and dreams. Occasionally, they went out to the movies, dancing, or dinner—rarely anything too fancy. Theirs was a simple joy of being with someone who wanted to understand you for who you were and who you wanted to become. They savored the pure contentment of knowing they belonged together, just the way they were, and would help one another grow and mature.

In only weeks, Christine understood Pete more deeply than she ever had known Bryan. They had fun together but also discussed the accident and the dark months following. Christine was forthright about her struggles with the guilt from her part in the accident and the anxiety that still clawed at her when she drove in the rain. She appreciated that Pete shared his own personal challenges caused by his time in Korea and by the lack of resources for the community program. Together, they dreamed of how to expand the job skills program and enable it to reach more people throughout the city.

By mid-January, Christine found a roommate, Diane, who was referred to her by Louise. On the first of February, she once again packed her belongings and moved out of her parents' house. Christine missed the close-knit time with her parents and Alice, but the small apartment was only a few minutes' drive away. She went over to her parents' house for supper each Wednesday evening. Pete joined the family occasionally but wanted to make sure that Christine and her family had time alone together as well.

One Wednesday evening after supper, Christine's mom made a point of telling Pete he was always welcome and wanted at the weekly meal. Dad chimed in that he appreciated having another man around when the women got to talking about clothing and accessories. Pete came more regularly after that. Christine treasured the fact that he seemed to enjoy and value spending time with her parents and sister.

Pete's family also invited the couple to supper and to watch his youngest brother, Todd, who was a junior at Arlington Heights High School, play basketball. Before the game, Eileen Ashby served delicious, hearty food. "The type that sticks to one's insides," as Christine's mom had always called it.

"Having three growing boys with healthy appetites makes a mother learn a few tricks to fill them and keep them from coming back to the kitchen all day and night," Eileen said with a laugh. She was as good-natured as John and Pete were. Christine felt like the Ashby family was quickly becoming as dear to her as her own.

The basketball game match up that evening was between Arlington Heights and their chief rival, Paschal High School. Christine loved attending football and basketball games in high school but had not been to one since graduation. Philip had run track and pursued academic and debate teams instead of the popular sports so there had been no real reason to go to the games.

Christine breathed in the familiar scent of floor wax and sweat as she entered her alma mater gymnasium. It transported her back to the days when she had cheered her team on during basketball games or sat in the bleachers for a school assembly or pep rally. Pete grabbed her hand and pulled her through the crowd to a spot in the bleachers. *I am definitely different from the untested youth I was while walking the school's halls.* Looking over at Pete, she believed that was not such a bad thing.

The basketball game this evening was an exciting one. The rival crowds were in the full spirit of rooting their team on to victory. It was a close game. Heights would be up for a time, then Paschal would regain the lead. Back and forth the players ran down the court, their shoes squeaking on the polished wood. Shot after shot swished through the air and into the basketball net. The boys from both teams were playing exceptionally well, their hearts clearly passionate about basketball and trouncing their long-standing competitor. Paschal made a comeback once again and all the fans roared, either in triumph or despair.

Christine looked out toward the other side's bleachers and was shocked to see the handsome face of Dennis Oswald. Although she had seen him just that one night and they had never met, Christine would recognize him anywhere. His features were striking with his strong jaw line and dark, brooding eyes which matched his slightly rumpled ebony hair that curled just above the collar. He sat next to a man with vibrant carrot-colored hair who was no doubt related to one of Paschal's players with the exact same shade of hair. Dennis was laughing and cheering Paschal's boys on like the rest of the crowd decked in purple and white.

Pete noticed her preoccupation and waited for Christine to share her musings. "That is Dennis Oswald over there by the man with the red hair and checked blazer," she whispered in his ear. They watched Dennis for a while longer. He appeared to be enjoying the game and talked familiarly with the couple and their children. Christine was pleased to know that Dennis was happy.

When the game ended, Christine took one last long look at Dennis. Instead of seeing a broken, defeated man crumpled to the curbside with his head in his hands, this is how she wanted to remember him: a man whose head was held high, laughing at life, and congratulating his team on their narrow victory. She pleaded with her mind to replace the tragic images of Dennis with these happier pictures, but knew that in the quiet of the night when it was between waking and sleeping, her mind would stubbornly refuse her simple request.

As the calendar pages turned, Christine continued to teach the business and office skills class and help students prepare résumés and apply for jobs. They had two more successful job placements in the first two months of the year. One local business even contacted Pete saying they had heard about the program and would be interested in being notified about candidates the program had trained. It was a small, but encouraging victory.

Another volunteer joined their team in February. Virginia was bilingual in English and Spanish, which enabled the volunteers to divide the students and teach both beginner and intermediate language learners with more success. After he and Christine had brainstormed about the program one night, Pete had written letters to a few leaders of other organizations like theirs. He had begun to receive letters and invitations to visit programs all over the country. He and John were able to meet with the leaders and attend meetings of programs in Austin, San Antonio, and even Oklahoma City. Together, the volunteers began incorporating some of the teaching practices and structure Pete and John had learned from the more established organizations. Christine could see how pleased Pete was with the program's progress and shared his excitement about its future.

Unfortunately, the group of volunteers faced some trouble too. One Tuesday night, they walked out to find that raw eggs had been thrown at all of their cars. Christine was a bit stunned by the callous behavior. Although Pete had warned her such incidents occurred in the past, it was the first time the harassment happened since she began volunteering.

Another week, Dave caught two teenage boys in the act of spreading nails about the parking lot when he went to his car to retrieve a book mid-meeting. Whoever it was wore dark clothing with their hats pulled low and a scarf around their faces. Pete decided to file a police report about both instances. The police could not find any clues to the identity of the men, but planned to send a patrol car by during the lessons in the coming weeks. They thought that the incidents were ramping up due to it being dark most of the time the classes were taking place.

"Those who set out to do petty crime usually do so under the cover of darkness when they are less likely to be seen and discovered," the police warned, reminding the volunteers to be vigilant of their surroundings and call if the need arose.

Each of the volunteers hoped the trespassers would stay away and counted down the days until the time change kept the sun up longer into the evenings.

The teachers were cheered once more by Paola's invitation for all of them to come to her daughter's quinceañera reception. On the night of the celebration, Pete dressed in his finest suit and Christine wore a dress of deep burgundy velvet. They were welcomed into Paola's home by her husband, Mateo Hernandez, and their large crowd of friends and family. The inside of the home was beautifully ornamented with brightly colored party décor and a banner honoring Paola's daughter, Antonia.

Christine found the traditional rite of passage celebration unique and special. Antonia wore a elaborate white dress and was as gracious a hostess as her mother. The crowd was lively and welcoming to Pete and the rest of the volunteers. Several people came to tell them how they appreciated the job skills program.

Mateo garnered the crowd's attention and blessed the meal after sharing a few words about Antonia. The celebratory supper was a feast to be sure. They started with pozoles before the main dishes were brought out. Christine and Pete tried empanadas, huaraches, tamales, and enchiladas. She found each dish to be flavorful and a wonderful mix of spice and savory. In the background, mariachis played traditional Spanish music. She and Pete enjoyed speaking with the Hernandezes' family and friends and learning about the rich culture of Mexico.

After supper, they headed outside to the backyard where a makeshift dance floor had been set up under trees strung with lights. Antonia and her court of honor began the dancing by performing a beautifully choreographed waltz. It was stunning to see the dancers swirl in time to the music and one another. The end of the dance was met with loud whistles and applause.

When the dance floor was opened for all to join, Pete and Christine watched to learn the steps, then joined in the fun. As they whirled around the floor, she noticed he held her close whenever he could. The entire evening had a magical feel to it. John and Eileen as well as the other guests from the program were caught up in the music and enthusiasm too. Christine caught glimpses of each of them dancing or laughing with other attendees.

When the violin's last note had faded in the moonlight, they hugged their gracious hosts and thanked them for including them in the celebration. They wished Antonia well before Pete took Christine home. It was a night she would never forget and she hoped their future would hold more friends who celebrated quinceañeras.

Bryan and Kathryn's wedding announcement and photograph splashed across the local section of the Fort

Worth Star-Telegram in late February. Christine stared at a copy in the office's lobby as she rearranged the paper on the waiting room coffee table. Bryan wore his best society-pleasing smile. He appeared engaged with the audience and hopefully this time he was. Christine wished them well and prayed for Kathryn's sake that they could cling to each other when life became tough.

"Christine, a moment of your time," Dr. Alan called, breaking through her musings.

Christine walked back to her desk and peered up at her boss. "Yes, sir?"

"Please add these notes to Mrs. Reynolds' file, and mark me down for vacation time the first week of June." He smiled and added, "I am going back home to South Carolina for a long overdue visit."

While Dr. Alan still unsettled her, Christine chose to see the good he had done. Due to his persistence, Dr. Bedford and Dr. Evans were able to reserve one day a week to work on paperwork and research instead of being overloaded with patients during the week and using their weekends to catch up. Dr. Alan had also convinced the other men to modernize the office equipment and their techniques. Christine had even been given a budget to redecorate the waiting room and reception area.

Christine and Margaret now spent their lunch hour and breaks poring over design magazines and interior décor books they checked out from the library. They finally settled on a pastel blue and beige color palette. The light blue and beige floral wallpaper was subtle and airy, with a touch of sophistication. They found gorgeous but durable beige chairs and a matching sofa to make patients feel like they were sitting in their own living rooms instead of waiting at the dentist's office. For weeks, poor Pete had listened to Christine debate the merits of different color combinations, paint finishes, wall paper patterns, furniture styles, and fabric upholsteries. Christine liked that he cared and asked questions and listened to her opinions. She told him so, which earned her a kiss.

On Valentine's Day, Pete hand-delivered a beautiful card with a special note; her favorite flowers, pink peonies; and a box of Whitman's chocolates on his way to work.

That night, they walked around the neighborhood for a bit after supper. Halfway around the third block, Pete stopped and took both of her hands in his. He waited until her eyes met his. The moon's bright glow lit his handsome face revealing his serious expression. "Christine, I hope it comes as no surprise to you, but I need to say it so there is no doubt how I feel. I love you. These past few months have been the best of my life because you have been in them."

Without hesitation Christine replied, "I love you too, Pete! You inspire and encourage me. You are faithful and supportive, and I can see how you truly care for me. I am so grateful to have you in my life."

He kissed her. Like everything Pete did, it was very well done.

They stood grinning at each other under the canopy of stars until the cold pierced through their jackets enough to send them on their way. How good it was to be cherished by a guy like Pete and to realize that he was a man she could trust with her heart.

As March approached, Christine began to feel anticipation and reticence warring within her. She would celebrate her twenty-third birthday on the fourth, and then, just ten days later, the first anniversary of the accident would arrive.

Christine talked to Pete, her parents, Patty, Sheila, her sisters, and Margaret about a way to honor Kay on the anniversary of the accident. Each tried to help Christine find a way to commemorate Kay Oswald. Lay flowers on the grave before sunrise? Would it bother Kay's family if they were not the first to adorn the grave? One of them suggested asking if she could have permission to place a cross or a marker next to the tree outside Frank's Diner, as some were known to do at the site of accidents. Christine did not feel enthused by the idea and decided against it.

Christine also wondered if she should try again to write the apology letter she had started to put into writing to Dennis many months ago. It had not felt like enough then, nor did it now. She had come to terms with the fact that nothing in the world would be able to make things up or replace what Dennis had lost. Seeing Dennis enjoying himself at the basketball game had brought relief to some degree. Maybe receiving the letter now would upset him more than if she allowed him to go on living without it. There was no way to truly know unless she asked him. She and Pete and her parents discussed the merits of finding and meeting Dennis in person. Christine did not want to foist herself upon the man if he had moved on or just wanted to forget that time in his life. Pete told her he would go with her if she decided it was the right course of action.

Grief and shame were tricky emotions. At times throughout the past eleven months, the emotions were like the Gulf of Mexico waves that swept her feet right from under her during a childhood visit to Galveston. The feelings startled her with their sudden appearance in the most unexpected circumstances and knocked her off balance. Other times, like a twining vine slowly creeping skyward—grasping, twisting, trying to take hold of her mind—the emotions subtly sought a foothold.

The decisions and the rollercoaster of emotions they brought on triggered her memories. Her nightmares began in earnest again. Somewhere in the dark edges of her mind, the dreams would form. Over and over, Christine would feel the terror of seeing a blur streak across her vision before she made impact and then lost control of the car. The sickening bump would jar her awake, sweat and tears drenching her pajamas.

As Christine examined her face in the mirror one morning, the dark circles under her eyes frustrated her, but she was at a loss as to what she could do besides cover them with makeup and press on. This time was not like those early days when she kept her emotions hidden. She now spoke openly about her feelings and fears and had processed them with the help of others as her pastor had recommended. Why then was she still facing the troublesome dreams? Why did she wrestle the emotions so often? What was wrong with her? When would she be able to truly move forward and fully heal?

Christine debated about packing a bag and moving home until she could get a hold on her night terrors but did not want to give up the ground she had gained or for Alice to lose precious sleep. Instead, night after night, she woke to a racing pulse and tried to stifle her screams or sobs in her pillow. Diane had been warned since the beginning of rooming together what Christine struggled with and faced. She was an evening shift nurse at the hospital, and on the nights she was home, Diane would heat a kettle of water and make tea when she heard the moaning and cries from Christine's room. Christine was grateful for the empathetic companionship as she sipped her tea and attempted to calm her frazzled mind.

When they met after work to spend time together, Christine could read concern in Pete's expression when he saw her. To his credit, Pete did not shy away from discussing any of her anxious feelings and fears. He would pull Christine close and ask her to talk about whatever came to her mind, be it good, bad, tragic, or typical. When she needed a distraction, he would regale her with stories about his work day and who he saw while traveling to and from or working at different job sites. Before leaving for home each evening, he hugged her and prayed over her while she wept against the front of his jacket. It was not a sustainable routine for either of them, but they drew emotionally closer and stronger as they pushed back the darkness together.

Christine hoped and prayed that once the anniversary of the accident passed, she could go forward in the same content manner that she had just two months prior. Mom gently reminded Christine that sometimes a person had to learn lessons through pain that never went away this side of the heavens. She added, that if one could learn to live through the trials or hurt and find joy despite of it, this person was victorious, more so than one who had never faced the testing of their spirit.

"Sometimes we do not understand why we, who believe and trust, still face challenges and despair even when we seek and follow the Lord. We find that answer in the book of James and in John chapter sixteen, sweet one. In this world there will be troubles, but we, who look to the Lord, can have peace through these trials."

Dad, too, counseled Christine to acknowledge that fears and despair could and would bombard her mind at times. He shared from personal experience how the onslaught could be often or every once in a while. He told her that a person cannot always prepare for or control the thoughts or situations they will encounter, but they can learn to control their reaction to them. Dad encouraged her to hold fast to what she knew to be true and use the techniques she had learned to help her through the tough moments.

Christine thought often about her parents' words. Maybe she would never be completely free of the memories and scars from the guilt, but could she have joy despite of them? Could she let her experiences change her for the better and grow her character instead of allowing them to overwhelm her and destroy her future happiness? *Yes, it has to be possible.* She could let God use the lessons she had been taught by heartache to bring peace throughout each day.

In Christine's opinion, March was Texas's best month. The short-lived though dreary winter weather was, for the most part, gone by March. In its place, spring began its magnificent show of color and light, a radiant combination with the scent of flower blossoms floating on the cool breezes. Bluebonnets and other wild flowers began to line the fields and roadsides. It truly was a sight to behold. She may have been partial because it was her birth month, but who was to say.

On her birthday the year before, Christine barely had a chance to go home and change after work before Bryan had rushed her out the door to dine at a table set for two in the center of Fort Worth's most expensive and upscale restaurant. It was a table where they could see and be seen by the restaurant's premiere guests—not exactly the romantic setting Christine imagined. They had spoken in soft, reserved tones to avoid disturbing other diners. Every so often, Bryan would correct Christine's etiquette or point out an elite patron in the restaurant. It had felt reminiscent of a work dinner between a boss and his employee instead of a birthday celebration. Several times throughout the meal, business associates had come to the table to greet Bryan. Christine had been ignored and excluded from the conversations for the most part and spent a great deal of the evening subtly examining the room's décor or the fashion of the diners around her.

Bryan had apologized the first time they were interrupted, but by the third instance, he was in the mood for conversation with others. He had even gone as far as to invite Judge Morton and his wife to join them without a thought or reference to the fact that it was Christine's birthday. Mrs. Morton had quickly bored of conversation with Christine and sat silently picking at her duck pate and watercress salad. Bryan's congeniality with his acquaintances made the evening run later than planned.

By eight o'clock, Christine had briefly excused herself to telephone her parents, sure that Bryan would assume she went to the ladies' room, if he thought of her at all. She'd hurriedly explained over the restaurant's phone that plans had changed and she and Bryan would not make it over to their house in time for cake that evening. Mom had told Christine she understood and that compromise was important if a relationship were to succeed.

Christine had asked to come the following day but made an excuse for Bryan because she doubted that he would want to be out two evenings in a row. Bryan ended the night with a soft kiss on Christine's forehead and a gift that his secretary had most likely chosen. Christine had been disheartened that she had not seen her parents on her birthday. It was a first in her entire lifespan that her father had not prayed his birthday blessing over her.

This year, Pete, her family, his family, Patty and Nelson, Margaret and husband, Louise, and Diane gathered together for a party in the Hinkles' backyard the Saturday before her birthday. The day was pleasant, sunny, and around sixty degrees: the perfect weather for a barbeque. They played corn hole and lawn croquet, two of Christine's favorite outdoor games. For supper, they ate smoked brisket with sides of potato salad, roasted corn, and fruit salad. Mom made a large chocolate birthday cake to celebrate. Dad summoned the crowd to gather around then prayed his birthday blessing over Christine and the coming year. While Mom lit the candles and the guests sang to her, she glanced around the yard. Each family member and friend in attendance was a blessing to her. She was content. She knew now that time with those she loved was one of the greatest gifts. This contentedness and gratitude were what she'd been missing in the past.

On her actual birthday, Pete made reservations at the restaurant of Christine's choice. They enjoyed a superb dinner before meeting Nelson and Patty for dessert. When he walked Christine to her apartment door at the end of the evening, Pete gave her a beautiful locket and grinned slyly, promising her that the locket was the first piece of jewelry he planned to give her this year but it most certainly was not the last. She was overjoyed by his hint and hoped he did not make her wait too long to receive it.

Chapter 16

March 1956

Dennis felt like he was being watched and possibly followed too. Normally, he was not a suspicious guy, but for the past week, he got a tingling sensation at the oddest times. He felt it last Saturday when he and Myrna sat out on her front stoop drinking their coffee as the day began, the tradition they had resumed now that the days were warming up again. It struck him again while walking across the bank lobby at work on Tuesday afternoon.

When he took Essie Mae out to dinner on Thursday night, that same sensation came rippling up his arm so strongly that he shivered a bit.

Essie Mae sent him a concerned look. She put her hand on his arm and questioned, "What is it, Dennis? You went pale just now. Are you feeling ill? Something has been bothering you for days. How can I help?"

He leaned close, not wanting the other patrons to be privy to their conversation especially if one of them was watching him. "I can't explain it exactly, but for days I have felt this presence watching me at the strangest times. I feel like I sound either egotistical or crazy, maybe a little of both. I'm a regular guy, not some Hollywood starlet. There is probably no basis to it. I might just be keyed up about the anniversary of Kay's death coming in a few days. Whatever or whomever it is, I wish they would reveal themselves or go away. I've had enough drama this past year to last me a lifetime."

Essie Mae's face was compassionate, but she told him she did not see anyone out of the ordinary and that she wished she could think of a way to ease his concerns. She assured him that she would be mindful of strange behavior from bank patrons or workers and be on the lookout when they were together.

On Saturday morning, there was a knock at Dennis's front door. He was not expecting Myrna, Essie Mae, or Leon until later and wondered who it might be. On the stoop waited a man who had a common enough face that was the type that blended well into crowds. Dennis revised that thought momentarily. The guy's furtive expression that dodged this way and that taking in his surroundings quickly gave Dennis reason to pause and be wary. His mind insisted he had seen the face before although he could not place it in a particular scene.

The man spoke. "Hello, Mr. Oswald, I have come to interview you for the paper."

"About what?" Dennis replied slowly, unsure where this conversation was going.

"Dennis, tell me how you are feeling these days. Have you moved on? Found another girl? Made friends at work?"

"What is this, pal? What are you aiming at?" Dennis allowed his voice to take on a stern, firm edge to it. *Why all the personal questions from a perfect stranger?* The unsettling sensation returned.

The man ignored Dennis's questions and shot back a few of his own. "Have you forgotten Kay and found another lover or do you cry yourself to sleep missing the wife you will never see again?"

Dennis resisted the urge to punch the guy in the jaw for his salacious suggestions. "Who are you and why are you here? Are you the one who has been following me around this week?"

The man shifted tactics but did not give up any ground. "Dennis, why don't I buy you a cup of coffee and we can talk. It could turn out to be profitable for us both."

"Why would I talk to someone who won't tell me his name and business being on my doorstep?"

"Fine." The man thrust out a rectangular card toward Dennis. "Here's my information. You call me if you want to discuss the accident or how it's been since then. I will give you ten percent of the profit if I sell the story. Tear-jerkers and sappy stories sell, pal."

"I'm not interested now, nor will I ever be," Dennis gritted out through clenched teeth. How could someone want to profit off the death of another or the heartbreak of those left behind?

"If you change your tune, we can meet for a cup of coffee at Frank's," the man said in his parting shot while walking down the sidewalk to a beat up Ford.

Dennis watched the reporter get in and zoom off with a roar of the engine and a cloud of exhaust in his wake. The business card read "Zachary Peoples." Dennis recognized the name and ran in to his room, where he pulled out the bottom drawer of their dresser. He pushed aside the wedding rings and cat pin that sat on top of three newspaper clippings. The first article gave a brief but honest description of the accident. The byline was not the same as the business card. The second story's author matched the name on the card.

Dennis had remembered being angered by Peoples' article. It was the interview Jolene had given the seedy reporter at Kay's funeral. The writing was lousy. Much of the article was fiction, made up in Jolene's mind, meant to play at the heartstrings of those gullible enough to believe it. It was an unhappy discovery he had made while searching for an article to send to Janet, explaining the accident so he would not have to. Why Dennis kept this trash, he did not know. There was no way he would give Peoples any more information.

Although the man never admitted it, Dennis bet it was Peoples who had been watching him all week. How else could he have known to ask certain questions this morning? If Dennis saw Peoples again, he would contact the police. He would also have to warn Essie Mae and Myrna. Who knew if Peoples was the type of guy to press innocent women to get the story he wanted?

As he went to shove the clippings back into their drawer, Dennis stared down at the final article. It was no bigger than the palm of his hand. He read over the familiar print of the short piece. The mortician who came to the hospital for Kay had asked if he wanted a staff member from the obituary section of the paper to contact him. Dennis had been out of his right mind the night of the accident but must have consented. Someone from the paper had called the next morning and asked him a few basic questions and told him they would mail him a bill. That was it.

Kay's brief, vibrant life had been summed up in thirty-seven words. She had not even been twenty-four years old.

Dennis sighed. He would be glad when the anniversary passed for more than one reason.

Wednesdays were ordinary days, the middle of the work week for many people. On Wednesday, March 14, Dennis rose early and dressed for the office just as he had done on this date the year before.

Essie Mae asked him how he was feeling on the ride in to the office. She listened to his brief answer and gave him a hug before they headed inside the bank. Martin met them at the door and reminded Dennis that he was nearby if he needed anything.

A number of his coworkers understood the significance of the day. They gave him sympathetic looks and several were brave enough to pat him on the back or whisper a word of encouragement or condolence. He was grateful for their efforts, no matter how great or small. Kindness was always a worthy gift to give.

Dennis took a half day off work, and so did Essie Mae, though she would lose money by clocking out early. They headed straight to Myrna's house. She fussed over Dennis and worked to entice him to eat a bit of lunch with cherry turnovers as bait. Dennis ate a few bites, mostly to appease Myrna, because he knew her kind efforts were meant to help. His tongue told him the food was delicious but his mind only registered ash. He felt off-kilter, unsure of what and how he wanted to feel this day.

For the rest of the mid-afternoon, Myrna and Essie Mae completed housework and light chores around him. Dennis played a round of checkers with Leon but neither his mind nor his heart was in the game. Leon took a nap on the couch while Dennis paced and deliberated about a plan to honor Kay this first anniversary.

It was ironic to him that he had spent weeks, months even, thinking about and trying to prepare himself for the day, and now that it was upon him, his mind was drawing a blank as to what course of action he should take. His brain recognized that he was over thinking it all in an effort to get things just right. That was no testament to Kay. She had lived for action and what she could get out of life. She chose what she wanted to do without a care whether it pleased others. If it were her, she would have chosen one of her favorite items to observe the day. A genuine idea began forming in his head. One that he felt Kay would be pleased by.

At three o'clock in the afternoon, Dennis had finally made up his mind about how he would commemorate Kay this day. He told Myrna and Essie Mae his plan and asked if they would join him. Each nodded soberly, and they set about readying themselves and Leon to leave.

Similar to the previous year, the rain clouds that had been forming as he and Essie Mae left the bank at noon were now brewing into a March thunderstorm. If the dark clouds were any indication, the storm promised to be a whopper. Lightning streaked the sky and thunder cracked from the heavens as they loaded into the car. It all seemed very fitting for the day.

Dennis ran his quick errand, and they were on their way again, the rain beating down on the windshield making it hard to see. The weather was so reminiscent of a year prior that it took his breath away for a moment. Dennis pulled off to the side of the road, and put his face in his hands attempting to block the unbidden images that flashed in front of his mind's eye. He could feel three sets of eyes peering at him.

"Dennis, are you all right? You don't have to push yourself. We are all more than happy to come back with you another day," Essie Mae said placing her hand on his shoulder from the backseat where she and Leon sat. Myrna sat in the passenger seat beside him, taking his hand in her own, patiently waiting for Dennis to decide what would come next.

"I want to do what I set out to do. This weather, it's so identical to that day that it threw me off for a minute. I'll be fine soon." After a minute or two more, Dennis started the car and carefully pulled away from the curb. The group was subdued as they made their way to the destination.

The evening preceding the anniversary of the accident Christine had given in to her need for comfort and had spent the night before at her parents' house. Her new roommate was understanding and kind, but this day, Christine needed the love and support her parents gave to bolster her through the hours ahead.

She insisted on going in to the office and completing her work day. All three dentists reminded Christine she had every right to take a personal day, but she persisted. She had to keep her mind and trembling hands busy.

The morning hours ticked by slowly. Some patients who knew her story sent her compassionate looks or tried to share a joke or encouraging word. A few were terse with her, but Christine no longer cared what they thought about the matter.

By three thirty that afternoon, Christine had attempted to type the same file three times and was emotionally drained. She was relieved when Mrs. Bedford entered the office a short time later and told Christine she would take over her duties for the rest of the day.

Christine left the office building only to remember that Pete had taken off time to drive her to work that morning. He planned to pick her up at four thirty, the time she had adamantly insisted on leaving at. Why had she been so stubborn? The clouds overhead threatened rain as she started to walk toward the bus stop down the block. Pete called her name from the edge of the parking lot.

"How did you know?" she said, relief coloring her voice.

"Elaine Bedford called your Mom before she headed to the office."

Christine was grateful to have so many friends and family looking out for her.

At the car, Pete gathered Christine in his arms and hugged her close. "Are you ready for this? Do you want to keep to the same plan we discussed last night?" He studied her closely as she answered.

"I am not sure that I will ever be ready, but I'm hoping it will bring some closure." He nodded and helped her into his work truck, explaining that he had not had time to pick up his car but wanted to get to her in time.

Pete and Christine stopped by a florist to get the item she had settled upon. As Pete helped Christine back into the truck, rain began to fall heavily just like the year before. She leaned back against the seat, closing her eyes. The searing throb in her throat returned for yet another visit, threatening to choke her. Pete held her hand tightly, patiently waiting with her. Christine met his eyes, nodding her assent to continue the pain-filled journey.

"Do you want to drive it or walk it?" he asked softly as they approached their intended location.

"Despite the rain, I think I had better walk it. I have avoided this road for a year, specifically going off the beaten path to side streets so I don't have to pass by. Today, I will walk it. Maybe another day I will get behind the wheel and cross the place of the accident, but I can't today."

They parked at the end of the block and grabbed an umbrella to share. Christine took a few steps forward and stopped as if waiting for a divine sign to continue. Then, as swiftly as the storm began, the sun broke through the clouds and the rain lessened to an occasional stray drop here or there. Christine peered around, absorbing the fresh, clean scent in the air after a rain shower. Could it be that God had answered her just now, reminding her that all storms came to an end in time?

She looked down the block and took note of how the street had changed in the past year and the ways it was still the same. The Dyers' dry cleaning and laundry was gone and replaced by a record store. There was a fresh coat of paint on the corner hardware store. Frank's Diner was still up ahead on the right, as was the thick, old oak tree her car bumped into after the initial crash. If one looked closely, there would be a gash in the trunk from her fender. The tree's scar was much like the one on her heart; the laceration had not killed either of them, but it would forever remain imprinted on a piece of them both.

Pete matched Christine's pace, never rushing, just a steady presence along the way. She slowed, then stopped a few feet past the bus stop. Pete gripped her hand securely, watching her face.

Christine gave him a nod and he handed her the bundle. One white rose for the innocent life taken, for the innocence of her life gone in one moment. Christine had cried hundreds of tears this past year. She had also been given redemption and joy. Kay Oswald could not come back from the grave, but Christine Hinkle could live her life in a way that honored Kay. She could choose a path that gave selflessly to her family and friends as well as others in her community. "A life that gives." This would be the motto, the passion behind how she lived and loved until she met her maker.

Christine squeezed Pete's hand, then pulled hers away. She scanned the distance both ways for oncoming vehicles, then crossed to the middle of the street to lay her parting contribution. When she got to the center of the road, she was surprised to see that one single red rose already lay there.

Dennis helped Myrna and Essie Mae from the car. The clouds were wringing out their last drops as he and Leon escorted the ladies down the block. He stopped when Frank's Diner was directly across. They gazed at the diner for a minute. Frank's had not changed a bit in the year since he had last laid eyes on it. The exterior of the diner had not altered at least; Dennis did not think he could ever step foot inside again. There were too many painful memories he did not wish to relive. He turned back to the small crowd. His people—a community he never expected, but was so thankful God saw fit to give him.

"Thank y'all for coming here with me today. I'm not sure where I would be without each of you. This scarlet rose is for Kay. She was so full of life and beauty. Red roses were her favorite flower." He looked for any cars coming a ways down the road each way and quickly hurried to place the rose near the middle of the road; then jogged back to the sidewalk where his friends waited for him. He hugged each of them tightly, trying to keep the tears in his eyes from falling. The group began to make their way back to the car when Essie Mae gasped gently, causing Dennis to turn to what her eyes were transfixed upon.

A woman. Christine Hinkle. He had seen her for only a few cognizant minutes that night, but he recognized her right away. The woman had just placed a flower upon his flower. She looked up and met his eyes, then quickly skittered back to the opposite curb. A young man protectively pulled her close while she stood gazing across at him. Dennis felt his feet propel himself forward; almost unknowingly, he checked again for oncoming cars and crossed the street once more. He approached the couple, but stopped when he was a few feet away.

"Christine Hinkle?"

Her pale face bobbed up, then down. Tear streaks were evident on her cheeks.

Dennis sent her a reassuring smile. "I want you to know I have forgiven you. I knew that night it was an accident. No one could have foreseen what happened. No one could have stopped it but God himself, and Kay wouldn't let Him. Please don't blame yourself anymore; I certainly don't."

Christine's tears began to fall in earnest, streaming down her face. At her consenting expression, Dennis tipped his hat and went back to embrace the people and the life he had come to love.

Christine and Pete watched Dennis Oswald lope across the street once more and take the hand of a pretty young woman. She smiled up at him, and they left with his little group.

Christine marveled at the forgiveness and grace Dennis offered to her so freely. It lightened her spirit. Dennis had given her the gift of redemption in his eyes. It was unexpected and so generous. She closed her eyes to praise the giver of ultimate redemption.

Then she turned to Pete. "My grandma always said, 'We can only walk forward through time. Best get to it.'"

Epilogue

1965

Although he knew what the answer would be before he posed the question, a few years into their marriage, Dennis asked Essie Mae whether she minded visiting the place of Kay's death each year when the anniversary came. She had held his face lovingly between her hands and waited until his eyes met hers to reply, "Never, my dear, sweet husband. I will not begrudge Kay that moment each year, ever."

And so, year after year, they made the trek to the accident scene. It had become a peculiar tradition of sorts to park on the east side of the street and walk down the block where she would watch Dennis place his crimson rose in the center of the road. Over the years, changes had taken place along the hallowed block and in their lives. The buildings and the tenants that occupied them altered as had the crowd that came with Dennis and Essie Mae.

Dennis and Essie Mae had married in the fall of 1956. Leon lived with them for a short time but with the addition

235

of another doctor establishing a new clinic in Graham, his parents felt it best for all that he come home to the farm to stay.

Dennis continued gaining more knowledge and leadership at Worthington National Bank. He was content to work hard and climb the corporate ladder as high as it would take him. In the summer of 1957, he and Essie Mae bought a little house of their own in a newly developed neighborhood, but faithfully drove Myrna to church each Sunday morning and stayed to visit with her in the afternoon. She was their biggest encouragement and prayer warrior until she passed away peacefully in her sleep just after the third anniversary of Kay's death.

Dennis and Essie Mae alone went to lay the rose down the next two years, all the while hoping and praying they could bring a new little life with them the following year. Five-month-old Sarah joined them the fifth year, her mother proudly pushing the baby carriage down the sidewalk. The subsequent year, Dennis carried one-year-old Sarah and Essie Mae pushed a two-week-old Russell in the carriage. Two years after that, little Wanda toddled alongside her older siblings on their trek to the "flower road" as Sarah had taken to calling it.

Some years Dennis placed his rose and they sat in the car a bit to see if Christine would come too. If she had not made it in time before they left, Dennis would circle back to the street later in the evening to check for the white rose. The single bloom was there each time. Crimson and white meeting once more. Dennis's heart warmed in gratitude.

Though Fort Worth was a relatively small town, Dennis had never seen Christine around except for these moments. He hoped one day to tell her thank you for her faithfulness to the memory of Kay. *Maybe this year*, he wished it to be truth as he stepped out of the car on the tenth anniversary.

Though it was considered late winter, in north Texas the spring-like weather was really showing off this year: blue skies with not a cloud in sight, a warm sun, and a hearty breeze to cool things down. The trees joined the competition with their brilliant-colored, beautiful blossoms set against bright green leaves.

Pete entered their house and washed the day's grime from work down the sink drain. He greeted Christine with a sweet, passionate kiss. She would never get over his goodness and the selfless love he offered her continuously throughout the years.

"Hello, how was your day?" he asked, waiting patiently for Christine's reply.

"It was good, all things considering. Mom had Charlie and I as well as Carol Ann and the kids over for lunch. Alice was able to sneak over for a bit on her lunch break, but Elizabeth could not make it due to little Paul having a cold. Charlie was a ham as usual, but he played well with his cousins; well, as gently as a three-year-old can. I picked up the rose from the florist on the way back. The kids are home from school and working on their homework." Pete was satisfied with Christine's report but still took time to read her face. He loved her so, his care evident in myriads of ways each day.

Christine returned his question, asking about how he was and how the work day went. They laughed at his dramatic retelling of a burst pipe in city hall that had one employee on the second floor thinking it was rain dripping from outside, so she sat at her desk under an umbrella. Pete did not understand her reasoning but asked the department head to have the roof checked soon.

Through the years, Pete had climbed the chain of command and more often than not found himself inside at a desk completing paperwork instead of being out on the job site with his fellow electricians. The pay was better though, and Pete was fulfilling his mission to make his city a better place for all its citizens. He told Christine he was happy, and she believed he meant it.

After a quick snack, the family loaded up in their station wagon and drove to the familiar spot. Christine held her flower ready as they walked down the sidewalk to stand in front of Frank's Diner. The diner was still going strong after all these years, although Frank and Shirley no longer ran the place. They had sold the diner and headed southeast to retire on the beaches of Florida, someone told Christine a few years back. The new owners must have decided to keep the original name and look to the place. Business seemed good. In fact, the place was highly recommended by many locals. Christine had not eaten there in over ten years and did not imagine she ever would again. The practicality when going to different events took Christine across this street occasionally, but she never lingered.

All day, Christine wondered if Dennis would make it again this year. Throughout the past nine years, he had been just as faithful to visit as Christine. When she saw him, he always parked on the side of the road across from Frank's while Christine and Pete parked on the opposite curb. Some years, they and their growing families would see each other in passing. She would wave or nod to him in acknowledgement. Other years, a crimson rose waited in the center of the street for her white bloom to join it.

Today, Pete held a squirming little Charlie in his arms with Jennifer and Sam standing closely beside him, as Christine cautiously approached the curb. She checked both directions and made her way to the center. Dennis stood there placing his rose on the ground.

For the first time in ten years, they had the exact same timing. He looked up at her, then glanced both ways for oncoming cars.

Dennis spoke first. "Christine, thank you for honoring Kay with me each year. I know that neither of us will ever forget her, and that, I think is the very thing she would want more than anything else in this world. To be known and loved and remembered always."

Christine nodded her head in agreement, uncertain of what to say. It was evident by the laugh lines on his face and his peaceful expression that Dennis had found joy and had a good life. It was exactly what she had hoped and prayed for him all these years.

Dennis smiled, "Have a great year!" Off he went to join the woman and children who awaited him.

Christine stepped back onto the sidewalk and into the arms of those she loved most.

"Mommy," her daughter questioned, "is that the man who forgave you?"

"Yes, sweet one."

"I like him."

"So do I."

And with that they headed home, never knowing where their path would take them next, but vowing to make each moment count.

About the Author

Mary Arnold has a Bachelor's degree in Education with an emphasis in Social Studies from Texas Christian University. As a teacher, she shared her passion for reading and history with her students. Mary is a native of north Texas. She enjoys spending time with her family and friends, reading, trying out various creative endeavors, and walking with her dog. *The Paths We Walk* is her first novel, which is set in a time period and city she loves.

Contact Mary at author.maryarnold@gmail.com
or find her on Facebook: Author Mary Arnold

Made in the USA
Coppell, TX
29 June 2022